RIPPLE EFFECT

Riley "Bear" Logan Book One

L.T. RYAN

Liquid Mind Media, LLC

DEDICATION

Special thanks to Amy, Barbara, Don, George, James, Melissa, and Phil.
And thank you to all of the Jack Noble and Riley "Bear" Logan fans out there! I can not express the gratitude I have for your support. I'm still amazed every day when I wake up and "go to work" with these guys.
If, by chance, this story is your introduction to the world of Jack & Bear, get your chores and work done now, then strap in, and hang on for the ride. It's a wild one!
~L.T.

THE JACK NOBLE SERIES

The Recruit (free)
The First Deception (Prequel 1)
Noble Beginnings
A Deadly Distance
Ripple Effect (Bear Logan)
Thin Line
Noble Intentions
When Dead in Greece
Noble Retribution
Noble Betrayal
Never Go Home
Beyond Betrayal (Clarissa Abbot)
Noble Judgment
Never Cry Mercy
Deadline
End Game

Receive a free copy of The Recruit by visiting http://ltryan.com/newsletter.

CHAPTER ONE

He sat across the street from the kind of fancy private school he never would have been able to attend when he was a teenager. It's not that his father hadn't had the money for it. Quite the contrary, in fact. But his uncle had forbid it. No member of the cartel was going to have that blight against their name.

Instead, he'd followed in his father's footsteps and gone to a run-down public school in the heart of the city. Fights in the cafeteria had made him a man. He grew up on the streets, learning which corners the cops avoided and which they hounded. It was a better, more useful education than any institution could provide. He was grateful, though he couldn't help the bitter taste that washed across his tongue. These kids that spilled from the tall entryway doors dressed in their matching uniforms had it so easy. They had no idea how advantaged they were.

But he wouldn't have traded his experience for the world. He could walk down any street and every single person in his way would step to the side. Even the biggest, toughest gangsters paid deference to him. It wasn't just his family name. It was the reputation he had built for himself. It was a reputation he was ready to flaunt.

He'd spent far too long in the shadow of his uncle.

"But that's about to change," he muttered. There was no one in the car to hear his words, but he didn't care. His eyes were trained on the girl who had just emerged from the front of the school. He brought his hand up to shield his eyes from the afternoon sun. A thin layer of sweat pooled where his index finger met his forehead.

She laughed and smiled and waved to her friends as she bounded down the front steps, looking carefree and optimistic. She was about to receive a hard lesson in life.

He was glad the windows on his sedan were so darkly tinted. The girl looked directly at him as she crossed the street and passed in front of his vehicle. But her eyes slid past the car and quickly returned to her book as soon as she made it to the other side of the road. A coy smile played around her lips as she read. She stopped at the corner, folded the corner of the page she was reading, and then continued on her way.

He checked his side mirror and studied the road. All clear. He slid out of his car and shut the door. It closed with a slight click. He doubted the girl was paying close enough attention that she'd be concerned by the sound in the first place, but he couldn't afford taking that chance. They had one shot to do this. If they missed their window, her father would go on high alert and they wouldn't have another chance at her.

She turned the corner, the wind rustling her school uniform, causing her plaid skirt to blow to the side. He kept an eye on the back of her head, determined not to let her out of his sight for one second. He tapped the screen of his phone and brought up his partner's contact info. He hit the call button, stuck his phone back in his pocket, and adjusted his earpiece.

The other man answered after the first ring. "Yeah."

"On my way."

"How long?"

"Three minutes." He looked over his shoulder. No one was following. "Maybe less."

"Copy."

They kept the line open, but neither one said anything for the next several minutes. He kept his distance from the girl by taking up a leisurely pace. He looked up at the buildings surrounding him, his hands deep in his pockets. He knew he didn't look like a typical gangster with his plain white sneakers, dark jeans, and brand new leather jacket. The people he passed on the street glanced at him for a second or two and then looked away. He was handsome, but not remarkable. They wouldn't remember him for more than a few minutes, if at all.

She stopped at the next corner and stole a glance at her paperback while waiting for a line of cars to pass. He cursed under his breath, but didn't slow down. It'd be too obvious he was tracking her if he mirrored her actions. She might be a young girl, but her father would've taught her the basics of keeping herself safe.

"What?" the other man asked.

"Passing it now," he said as he walked by the girl. She smelled like lavender shampoo. It stood out amid the lingering exhaust fumes.

She looked up from her book at him for a second. There was no sign of recognition on her face. The fear she should feel was not present.

The other man cursed. "Still on track?"

"It'll be fine."

The line went silent again. He didn't worry too much. They'd been watching for a while now. They knew the route the girl took from school each and every day. Unless something came up, they'd know exactly where she was heading. It didn't much matter if he was in front of her or behind her.

The sound of sneakers tapping the sidewalk behind him indicated that she'd started walking again. He slowed down enough that she was only a few paces behind. When they got to the end of the block, he was afraid she'd stop again and it'd put him even further out in front, but she didn't even pause at the corner.

"Incoming," he said quietly.

This street was the quietest one they had found on her route home. It also happened to have a couple alleyways along the way. The buildings were tall and close together here, which meant plenty of shadows to hide in.

He passed by his partner's hiding spot and caught the other man out of the corner of his eye. He was pressed against the wall, where the girl would only be able to see him once it was too late. As long as he grabbed her and wrapped a hand around her mouth right away, no one would notice the girl being snatched right off the street. The road was empty. The windows in the building across the street closed and boarded up.

He felt his pulse quicken now that they were on the precipice of success.

There was a small scuffle behind him, but it was nearly a silent one. He slowed down and looked around him. The street was deserted. He turned back to the alley just as one of the girl's stark white shoes disappeared into the darkness. He checked their surroundings one more time and, certain that no one was watching, followed her into the alley.

It took a moment for his eyes to adjust now that he was out of the bright sunlight. Once they did, he saw the other man struggling to hold onto the tiny girl. She was lean and not particularly strong. How many ten-year-olds were? Still, she was flailing enough that his partner was having trouble keeping her in his arms.

He rushed forward and grabbed her feet. One hand only had hold of her sneaker laces. She yanked her foot back, untying her shoe in the process. She managed to drive her knee into his stomach as he reached again for her foot. It knocked some of the wind out of him, but not enough to slow him down. He crossed her ankles and held them against his side with one arm. With his free hand, he reached into his pocket and pulled out a knife. He flicked it open and pointed in her direction. She instantly stilled.

"Good girl," he said. "Behave and nothing will happen to you."

She nodded, tears forming in the corners of her eyes. They spilled over the edge and cascaded down her cheeks.

The other man pulled her further into the alley and pushed her up against the brick wall, his hand covering her mouth.

He placed the knife under her chin. "You scream, you die. Understand?"

The tears were nonstop now, but she nodded her understanding. The two men stared at each other. They didn't need words to communicate. When the other guy released her, the girl followed the movements of his hands. Her eyes widened when he pulled a small roll of duct tape out of his jacket pocket.

"Please," she whispered, the sound choked by her sobs. "Please don't hurt me."

"Don't do anything stupid and we won't," he said.

"I have money. I can get more from the ATM. If it's money you want, I can give you everything I have."

"That's not gonna do the trick for us, sweetheart."

"Please." Her lip wobbled. Her voice came out watery and strained. "Please let me go."

The other guy ignored her pleas and slapped the tape over her mouth. When she tried to shrink away from him, he reminded her of the blade under her chin. She froze and allowed the other man to smooth the tape over her lips. He heard her whimper, which made him smile.

His partner moved on to her hands, wrapping them tightly together with the duct tape. When he started to bind her ankles, she twitched as though she wanted to kick him and attempt to make her escape. One look down at the blade and she stilled. It wasn't worth the risk.

When the job was done, he brushed her hair out of her face and put the knife away. "If everything goes according to plan, you'll be seeing your father again soon enough."

The tears continued to fall down the girl's face as they picked her up, one on each end, and carried her down the alleyway and into one of the warehouses where they had a commercial van waiting to take them to the next location.

CHAPTER TWO

March 21, 2006

The little Italian joint in Miami was the perfect place for a meeting between spooks. Customers didn't linger during the middle of the day. The workers didn't pay much attention. A deal to take a life could be cut in a couple of minutes and no one would be the wiser.

Jack and I were there to meet an associate of an associate. Details hadn't been provided in the initial communication. They never were. Some guys prefer to meet in a hotel room or out on a deserted road. Not us. We preferred public places for these kinds of deals.

"This pizza better be damned good, Bear." Jack rubbed at his eyes with his thumb and forefinger, still recovering from his redeye in from New York.

"It's pizza." I twisted around in my seat to look at the door leading to the kitchen. I caught a peek of a stainless-steel rack with brown cardboard boxes stacked on each shelf. The top stack almost touched the ceiling. My stomach was rebelling against me, and the only thing that would quell its anger was half a pie. I shifted back. "You can't screw up pizza."

"You sure as hell can," Jack said. "There's good pizza and there's bad pizza, just like everything else. All I'm saying is this better be good pizza."

"There's good pizza and less good pizza," I said. "Dough, sauce, cheese, toppings. You can't screw that up."

"You vastly underestimate people's idiocy, Bear."

"And you overestimate your ability to hold your liquor, Jack."

"When in Miami." He took several gulps of water.

"You've only been here—"

My retort was cut off as the waitress stopped in front of us. She was a cute brunette who kept her eyes on Jack. She slid the pie onto our table and placed a pair of plates in front of us, along with a stack of napkins.

"Anything else?" she asked Jack.

"Another water for my friend," I said. Jack gave me a look. I lifted an empty shaker off the table. "And how about some extra parm?"

"You got it." She smiled down at Jack, then turned on her heel and hurried away.

He finished off the last of his water. The ice cubes rattled as he set the cup on the table. He leaned back in his seat and stretched. Joints cracked like a tire rolling over bubble wrap. His gaze kept shifting to the entrance. Our contact was late, and that didn't sit well with either of us.

"Here you are," the waitress said, sidling up to our table and placing a fresh glass of water in front of Jack.

"And the cheese?" I shook the final remains of the previous container onto my slice.

"Oh, right." She glanced at me for the first time. "Right away."

I shook my head after her, but occupied myself with shoving my second slice into my mouth. "You gonna eat?" I asked Jack around a mouthful of food.

"Yeah, yeah." Jack slid a piece onto his plate. "You're such a nag today, man."

"You're just extra sensitive." I pulled a third slice toward me.

I chuckled, but the clang of the bell at the front of the shop made me pause mid-bite. Three men entered the pizzeria, their gaze sweeping over the patrons until they reached us. They paused on Jack and me for only a second or two. Long enough for a trained eye to notice, but no one else in the place paid the new customers any attention.

"Know them?" Neither of us sat with our backs to the door, so we both saw the members of the group as soon as each one walked in.

"No," I said. "You?"

He shook his head. Neither one of us acted outwardly concerned, but all our attention was now on the men walking toward us.

"Must be new guys," I said. "Frank's getting sloppy."

"Well no one was bound to be as good as us."

I tipped my head in his direction, watching as the third guy pulled out a pack of cigarettes as he scanned the room one more time, and then stepped back out through the door. He cupped his hand around the end of the stick, and soon smoke wafted up into the air, sucked into the restaurant through the cracked door. The man leaned his head back and blew a stream upwards into the sky. A moment later he walked across the street and leaned against a tree. He remained posted there, looking through the front window of the restaurant.

The other two walked through the center of the room, avoiding eye contact with us. The second one had red hair and an unfortunately matching mustache. He stopped off at the bar and raised a hand to order a drink. I spotted his piece on the back of his right hip under his t-shirt. Didn't look like he cared to conceal it. The bartender pulled out a glass and set it in front of him.

The third man had shortly cropped dark hair and still had on his sunglasses. He walked up to our table, slid out a chair, and sat down. When he reached for a slice of pizza, Jack grabbed the guy's wrist and turned the guy's fist back on himself.

"What can we help you with?" Jack said.

"Just wanted to drop in and say hi. Name's Daniel Thorne."

"People like us don't drop in." Jack released the guy's arm and leaned back again.

"How's our mutual friend?" I didn't bother introducing myself. Thorne would know who we were. And what we were capable of.

"Impatient." Thorne rubbed the red mark on his arm while looking Jack up and down. "You look like shit."

"Hangover and a late flight," Jack said. "What's your excuse?"

I laughed loudly. A few heads turned, but no one paid us any attention. They turned back to their food and drinks.

Thorne shifted uncomfortably in his seat.

I leaned over my arm toward the guy. "You know, you're drawing more attention to yourself wearing sunglasses inside than if we got up on the table and started dancing."

"It wouldn't hold your weight, big man," Jack said. "Sorry to break it to you."

I twisted my face into mock offense. "Whatever could you mean, Jack?"

Thorne sighed and took off his glasses, folding them up and placing them on the table in front of him. "You know, I thought meeting the infamous Jack Noble and Riley Logan would be a bit more climactic. Don't meet your heroes, I guess."

"Aw, Bear." Jack placed a hand over his heart. "We have fans."

The waitress chose that time to finally bring me my parmesan. She looked the new guy up and down, seemed unimpressed. "Should I bring out another plate?"

"Nah," Jack said. "Our buddy here was just stopping by to say a quick hi. He won't be staying."

Thorne clenched his jaw and looked between me and Jack, but he didn't say anything. He stood up and unzipped his jacket. He wasn't stupid enough to try something in public, but both of us kept an eye on Thorne's movements just in case. Jack had a habit of getting under people's skin.

"Bathroom?" Thorne asked the waitress, laying his jacket down on the table.

"Back through here." She led him away.

"Where the hell does Frank get these guys?" Jack asked.

"Probably the same place he got you." My gaze swept around the pub once, noting the man drinking at the bar watching us from the mirror, as well as the guy who was still smoking outside, still leaning against the same tree. He brought his fist up to his mouth in a fake yawn and looked away. I reached for the jacket and pulled it onto my lap, feeling the weight of an envelope drop into my hand. I tucked it into my own coat pocket and swung Thorne's jacket around the back of his chair.

Jack pushed his plate to the middle of the table and watched as I pulled out enough cash to cover the meal and a decent tip. I led us out, passing the red-haired man and ignoring the way he stared daggers at us. It seemed we weren't popular with any of Frank's men these days.

Jack gave the guy across the street a mock salute and then tossed on a pair of sunglasses.

I looked at him out of the corner of my eye. "Did you steal those from Thorne?"

"Borrow, big man," Jack said. "I borrowed them from our new friend."

"Borrowing implies the intention of returning them."

"Oh, I absolutely have every intention of returning them," Jack said. "I can't wait to see our new friend Thorne again. He seems like a fun guy."

"You could use a little less fun, Jack," I said. "How's that hangover treating you?"

"Cured," Jack said.

"Told you the pizza would be good."

"I've had better."

"Still good though."

"Where are we heading?" Jack pointed at my jacket.

I reached into my pocket and pulled out the envelope, sliding the papers out halfway and skimming the dossier. "Take a guess."

"Argentina," Jack said immediately. "Rogue military faction."

"You owe me a beer." I handed him the papers. "Costa Rica. Corrupt politician."

CHAPTER THREE

March 23, 2006

I stared out across the beach, watching the waves roll in at a steady rhythm that kept time with my heartbeat. I took a pull from my bottle, barely tasting the light beer as I allowed the sound of the ocean to overtake my thoughts and relax me.

Frank's dossier was straight to the point. We were in Costa Rica to deal with a corrupt politician named Thomas Goddard. Goddard had developed a habit of visiting the country to take care of his various cartel dealings in person. He'd visit at least once a quarter, sometimes more, and stay up to two weeks at a time. Tax dollars hard at work. Some misdoings were overlooked. But Goddard was drawing too much attention to himself, and the price of making a mistake like that was death.

Jack and I were tasked with executing the punishment.

Javier Torres, a long-time intelligence agent in Costa Rica, was our point of contact for the operation. He knew Goddard's comings and goings, and would be the man to set us up for the job. Intel, weapons, cover ups. He'd assist in every way. We'd be meeting him later that day to get more information.

A peal of laughter broke my concentration. I glanced over my shoulder and across the open-air bar to where Jack stood talking to one of the locals. She was tall, maybe five foot eight or so, with bronze skin and dark eyes and hair to match. She had one hand on Jack's chest, and he had one hand on her waist. The other tucked a strand of windblown hair behind her ear.

The woman leaned forward and whispered something into Jack's ear, then kissed him on the cheek and sauntered away. Jack stood, admiring after her for a long moment before jogging back over to me with a grin on his face.

"Where's your phone?" Jack asked.

"What?"

"Your phone, your phone," Jack said, waving for me to hurry up. "Before I forget her number."

"Quit messing around, man." I lifted my bottle to my mouth before realizing I had already drained the last drop. I gave up and placed my phone on the table where he snatched it up. "We've got to meet Javier in two hours."

"We might have time." Jack sat down and looked past me to where the woman had walked off.

"Remember the last time you had some fun?" I signaled for the check. "We need to stay on top of this one."

"I plan to." A smile spread across his face. When I didn't laugh, he shook his head and leaned back in his chair. "All right, then. Where're we heading?"

"The mountains."

I rented an older white Range Rover that took us slowly but steadily up to the peak of a nearby mountain. The road was narrow and winding and once we had to scrape by an oncoming car to get through a narrow pass. Considering the Rover was already pretty banged up, I figured the car company was used to visitors making similar mountain treks.

But no visitors would make the trip to Javier's office. By the time we reached the cinder block building the road was nothing more than a couple of pencil-thin slits of dirt in overgrown grass. The air was so thin that both of us had a little trouble breathing.

Jack lifted his sunglasses to the top of his head and stared across the gravel lot to the building. "Homey."

I grunted in agreement. The building was nothing more than concrete block and a steel door. It would have looked abandoned and forlorn had there not been a couple late model sedans parked out front. Still, the building sucked the vibrancy out of the lush jungle surrounding it.

"This place doesn't exactly boost morale," I said. "Guess not many workplaces do, though."

"We just supposed to wait?" Jack checked his side mirror. Javier was an asset, but that didn't give us an excuse to get complacent.

No sooner had I nodded my head than the door clanged open and Javier strolled out to meet us. He was a lean man, in his mid-30s, with flecks of grey in his hair. He was wearing a tailored dark-blue suit. His while collared shirt was unbuttoned at the neck, and he'd forgone the tie today. He looked calm as he stepped up to our vehicle, pausing a moment to scan the trees around us. Then Javier's gaze settled back on the two of us, sizing us up before he nodded his head.

Jack and I exited the Land Rover at the same time and followed Javier as he turned and walked back into the building. Jack checked over his shoulder one more time and appeared to be satisfied that we weren't being watched from the surrounding forest. I kept my eyes on the back of Javier's head until we were through the door and into the main entryway.

It took a few seconds for my eyes to adjust from the bright sunlight outside to the dim, artificial lighting inside. The entryway was bare bones, with only a simple metal desk in one corner and a single padded chair in the other.

"Don't get many visitors, huh?" Jack said.

"We try to avoid them, yes." Javier paused at the secretary's desk. His accent was light.

I took note of the receptionist, an older woman with dyed red hair. She had to have been in her mid-50s, and looked like she was still living in that era. Her hair was done up in a beehive, her nails were long and painted crimson, and she wore a string of pearls above a turquoise dress that showed off her ample cleavage. I wondered how long she had worked there, and who she was trying to impress.

The woman didn't bother looking up when the three of us passed. When Javier spoke to her in rapid-fire Spanish, she pulled out a pen and a pad of paper and began to take notes. She nodded her head once, twice, three times, and by the time Javier was done speaking, she had a page full of notes and her fingers were already flying over the keyboard.

Jack looked over at me, knowing I understood every word Javier had said. I shook my head subtly. It wasn't anything important. A light was out in one of the offices and there was a leaky faucet in the men's bathroom.

Javier led us down the spiraling set of stairs. Bringing up the rear, I took note of the way Javier moved, the way he set his shoulders and carried himself. His body language stayed neutral, calm even. I wasn't sure why I was looking for signs that this thing would go sideways. By all accounts, it was a pretty straight forward op.

When we hit the first platform and ventured out into the office space below the reception area, I realized how big the facility was. That's what was great about a place like this. The entrance was a single room with two points of egress—the main door and the staircase down to the next level. If there was any trouble, the receptionist would alert those below, who could easily defend their office space by trapping any intruders in the staircase.

The hallway stretched before us. My eyes finally adjusted to the light. It also helped that the fluorescence down here was much brighter. The only windows to the rooms that dotted the hallway on each side were a sliver of glass set into the doors, each of which had their own keypad. Javier walked us past a dozen before we turned a corner, only to find a dozen more in either direction.

"Jesus," Jack muttered. Then he raised his voice. "How big is this place?"

"Big enough." Javier stopped in front of a door seemingly at random and punched in a ten-digit code. He blocked our view with his body. The keypad was silent. There was no way we could guess the numbers from the sound alone.

We followed him inside a spacious office. He flipped a switch on the wall and overhead lights flickered to life. The room was surrounded by concrete, and there were no windows, but the rich oak desk and a couple of plump red chairs with a matching carpet made it feel less cold than the rest of the floor. Maybe all the rooms looked like this. They kept it that way for the sanity of their agents.

"Love what you've done with the place," I said.

Javier nodded. "Please, sit. Let us begin."

Jack and I sat down, sinking into the chairs with a sigh. The trip in the Rover had been a bumpy one, and Javier's office was warm and comfortable. Felt like a cave. I realized how tired I was for the first time all day.

I sat up straighter in the chair. If I wasn't careful, I'd probably fall asleep. "What have you got for us, Javier?"

"Thomas Goddard." Javier pulled a file from his desk and opened it up in front of him. "He is a senator in the United States government who visits Costa Rica several times a year. While he is here, his schedule is fairly routine." He held out his hand and tilted it side to side. "He eats breakfast and lunch at the same times and same places each day. He is usually accompanied by a contact, but if he does not have a meeting that day, he is accompanied by a woman. Some of them show up more regularly than others. He doesn't seem to have a favorite among them. Dinner is more of a social event, where he is joined by several high-profile Costa Rican politicians or actors. This usually occurs around nine, again at the same restaurant each night. Oddly enough, he often stays in a condo suite in town even though he owns a place further away. This, I'm sure, is not known by many people."

Javier handed me the folder so I could scout the restaurants in question and check out their locations in relation to one another. The senator didn't stray far within the city limits of San José, at least not during mealtimes.

"What about when he's not eating?" I passed the folder to Jack.

"During the day, he is either near a beach or secreted away to meet with his cartel contacts."

"Near a beach?" Jack asked, looking up. "Working on his tan?"

"As a matter of fact, yes." Javier's lips twitched, perhaps the closest he could get to a smile. But then his demeanor became neutral again. "But don't underestimate Goddard. He is cunning and dangerous and has no remorse. Even when he's not the one who pulls the trigger, he is usually the person behind it."

CHAPTER FOUR

Thomas Goddard's alarm clock went off at five in the morning every day, even on weekends. He never used the snooze and he never laid in bed after he turned his alarm off. He hit the button, and five seconds later his feet hit the ground. Goddard stretched with a couple sun salutations, freeing the last remnants of sleep from his mind.

Then he went to work.

Goddard enjoyed routine. He liked to know what to expect and he liked the feeling of accomplishment when he checked each item off his mental to-do list. Some people didn't understand his rigid behavior, but they couldn't argue with the results. It had gotten him to where he is today—a seat in the Senate. Not to mention the almost monthly trips to Costa Rica.

By the time Goddard had completed his workout it was only a few minutes past six. He took the stairs back up to his room where he showered and dressed for the day. Sitting down at the table in his suite, his assistant placed *The Washington Post*, *The Wall Street Journal*, and *The New York Times* in front of him, along with a hot cup of dark roast coffee. Dark roast for the flavor and slightly reduced caffeine.

"Thank you, Jordan." Goddard sipped from the mug, enjoying the way the hot liquid warmed his throat and stomach. He didn't indulge in much, but coffee was one exception. Women were another. "What's the news?"

"Not much today, sir," Jordan said. He already had his PDA out and was scrolling through his notes. "Jeffries is still stalling on the pipeline, though Winston and Vega have come around. The Canadians are still hesitant, but I've heard that the appropriate incentives are being offered."

"Good, good." Goddard absorbed the information, but allowed his mind to focus on the papers in front of him. "Anything else?"

"No, sir."

"Call me just before seven," Goddard said.

"Yes, sir." Jordan turned on his heel to leave.

Goddard finished up the *New York Times* just as his phone rang. He told Jordan to meet him down in the lobby in five, though he suspected his assistant was already waiting there. Jordan wasn't much for conversation, not that he minded, but he was an excellent employee. He was never late, he often anticipated Goddard's needs before he voiced them, and most importantly, he never asked questions. He was a young man, much younger than Goddard, but he suspected Jordan grew up in a household that had required him to mature quickly. Whatever happened there, it was to Goddard's benefit.

Goddard, his assistant, and his small security detail swept into Café Flores and sat at their usual table, which was always reserved for the senator when he was in town. The staff knew him to be a steady customer who was not to be disturbed during his meals unless he signaled for them. And if they kept up with his demands in a timely manner, he would tip them more than they'd make the rest of the day combined.

Señor Vasquez was waiting patiently at the table when they

arrived. He stood up and shook the senator's hand, nodded to Jordan, and swept a careful eye across the three men in Goddard's security detail. Satisfied that none of them were itching to reach for their concealed weapons, Vasquez sat down and waited for Goddard to speak first.

Goddard nodded to his guards, who left the café after one final look across all the patrons. Jordan retreated to another table, still within earshot, but well enough away to not be intrusive.

A waitress came by with two cups of coffee and a plate of eggs and toast for Goddard. When she asked Vasquez what he'd like to eat, he shook his head.

"Breakfast is the most important meal of the day, Señor," Goddard said, scooping his eggs onto his toast. "You should eat something."

"You pay too much attention to cereal commercials," Vasquez said. "It's all a big lie, you know. Anyway, coffee is fine for me." Vasquez's accent was light—a product of growing up in Florida. He had been a former lieutenant for the Miami-Dade police. Now he was a private investigator who had his hands in a surprising amount of dealings. Former police officers always made the best investigators. They had the training, the contacts, and the instinct to get their guys. Throw in ambition and a strong love of family, like Vasquez had, and that line between right and wrong blurred just enough to make him useful to Goddard.

"Very well," Goddard said, as the waitress walked away. She would have no other tables to wait on this morning, ensuring they received the best service. "How are your grandchildren? Jasmine and Rafael, if I remember correctly?"

"Yes, sir," Vasquez said. "Very well. Jasmine turns ten tomorrow."

"Ten!" Goddard exclaimed. He was genuinely delighted. His grandchildren were another one of his indulgences. "My Rachel is closing in on eight now. She's terrified of turning ten. Thinks she'll be a completely different person."

Vasquez smiled and nodded. "Funny, the things that get into their heads."

"Jordan," Goddard said, not bothering to take his eyes off Vasquez. He knew his assistant was listening. "Have a gift sent to Vasquez's daughter's house. Something that won't annoy her too much. We don't need any singing ponies repeating the same song over and over until the child is bored with the toy."

"Yes, sir," Jordan said.

Goddard could feel the way the tone shifted between him and Vasquez. On the one hand, it was a kind gesture between friends to send someone's granddaughter a gift for their tenth birthday. On the other hand, it was a subtle reminder that he knew where Vasquez's granddaughter lived should anything be amiss with the information he received today.

"Thank you." Vasquez's voice was neutral, but Goddard saw the calculated way he raised his coffee to his lips in an effort to bite back another remark. Vasquez wasn't the kind of man who normally took orders from others, but Goddard happened to be in an excellent position to command respect and fear. Vasquez knew his place.

"What have you got for me today, Señor?" Goddard asked.

Vasquez settled into his seat. This was easy territory. This was what he was good at. "Mateo Martinez has a mole in his operation that he doesn't want you to know about."

Goddard paused with his coffee halfway to his lips. "How big of a mole?"

"For now it seems to be under control."

"For now." He put his cup down without taking a sip.

"Martinez is dealing with the problem, but he's having trouble doing it quietly. Rumors are spreading that he's losing his grip on the operation. Some others are looking to move in."

"That doesn't sound like under control to me. Do you know who the mole is?"

"Nicolás Garcia. Young, rash, stupid. But he has clout. His father was a high-ranking officer in the cartel, but he was killed several years ago."

"So Garcia has something to prove."

Vasquez nodded. "He's looking to make waves, and he thinks killing Martinez is the best way to do that. He wants to lead the operation, get rid of the gringo influences, and make more money."

"More money?" Goddard laughed. "Without me? He *is* stupid."

"He has some support," Vasquez offered.

Goddard waved away the concern. "People are temperamental. Gangsters and criminals even more so. Are you sure Garcia is the one behind the leaks?"

"Positive." Vasquez had a challenging look in his eyes that Goddard liked.

"I believe you, my friend," Goddard said. "Very well. I'll instruct Mateo on what to do."

"There is one problem." Vasquez paused. "Nicolás is Mateo's nephew. He will not like the idea of killing his own blood."

"And in that case, I assume you have some proof?"

Vasquez nodded and pulled a small envelope from his pocket. "This is everything I've gathered on Nicolás's comings and goings. He's met with several other drug lords over the last few months. He remains loyal to his uncle's cartel, but he has given them enough information to cause trouble with shipments."

"So he wants to rock the boat, but not sink it." Goddard tucked the envelope into his jacket. He would study it later before his meeting with Mateo. "That's a fine line to walk."

"It is," Vasquez said. "Nicolás may not be the smartest member of Mateo's cartel, but some of his supporters have been playing the game for some time. If they can keep Nicolás's temper in check, they'll likely succeed in getting rid of Mateo."

"And leaving Nicolás in as a figurehead?"

Vasquez shrugged. "Figureheads don't last long in situations like this."

"Either way, Nicolás Garcia's days are numbered. Is there any benefit to letting this play out?"

Vasquez drained his coffee cup before he answered. Goddard could see the wheels spinning in his mind. The senator had been dealing in this business long enough to have a feel for how situations like this would play out, but he was a careful man. There was no harm in getting a second opinion, especially one from the likes of Vasquez. He had a knack for knowing which side to align himself with. For a long time, it was with the police force. Now, it was usually on the other side of that line.

"Mateo is a good drug lord. He is strong without drawing too much attention to himself. He has more supporters than Nicolás, some of which would remain loyal to his name even after the takeover. That goes a long way. Garcia is a hothead, and he has a silver tongue. He's charismatic, but he doesn't know how to play a long game. He'd put a bullet in your head just to prove a point, even if it meant watching his empire crash down around him."

Goddard signaled the waitress for the check and returned his attention to Vasquez. He could see where this was heading, and knew something had to be done sooner than later. Though he also knew a shakeup could be of some benefit to him.

"You are doing well with Mateo," Vasquez said. "It is my recommendation to continue working with him. Tell him about Nicolás and see what he does. More than likely he'll kill him, but if he does not..."

"Then I'll know it's time for some change." Goddard smiled up at the waitress as she approached and handed her a wad of cash. She beamed at him and quietly said thanks, retreating quickly as if the money would disappear if she didn't pocket it right away.

Both men stood and shook hands, with Vasquez making a quick exit out the front. He passed by Spero, Goddard's security detail team leader, with a nod of his head, but the American paid him no attention as he approached his boss with a determined look on his face.

"What's wrong?" Goddard asked. Jordan was by his side in an instant.

"Nothing, sir," Spero said. "We thought we'd take you out the back today."

Goddard wiped his mouth with a napkin and threw it down on the table. "I doubt it's for a change in scenery."

"Precaution, sir." Spero waited until another one of his men joined them at the table, and then Spero led Goddard and Jordan through the kitchen with the other man taking up the rear.

"Very well," Goddard said. He trusted Spero with his life, but the man was borderline paranoid. Then again, that's probably what had kept Goddard alive all these years.

Spero spoke into the mic on his lapel. "Perimeter secure?"

The answer must've been in the affirmative because he told the small group to move out.

Goddard turned back to Jordan, who was calm despite the potential threat. "If this all plays out according to plan, be sure to send something for Vasquez as thanks."

"Yes, sir." Jordan swiped at his ever-present PDA. "And if it doesn't go according to plan?"

Goddard liked Vasquez. He hadn't let him down yet, but there was always time for someone to screw up. He'd have to send the man a message, but he didn't believe he needed to have him killed. Then again, that depended on how badly it went.

"We'll play it by ear," Goddard told his assistant.

CHAPTER FIVE

I knew I'd been spotted as soon as the bigger security guard turned to the other and nodded his head, then proceeded to enter the café where Goddard was having lunch. The smaller of the two guards stood firm and scanned the street. He paused on me as I turned the corner into an alleyway and pulled out my phone.

"Yeah?" Jack answered.

"Pretty sure I've been spotted."

"Not like you, big man."

"I know, I know." I peeked around the corner toward the café and ducked back before the guy spotted me again. "These guys are jumpy. They're definitely on the lookout."

"Think it's for us?"

"Can't imagine how they'd have picked up on us already," I said. "Maybe they're just good at their jobs."

"Go figure. What now?"

"Hang on." I leaned around the corner again, just in time to see the smaller security guard step to the side and allow another man to exit the café. He had tanned skin and a hard face. The way he carried himself told me he had once been a part of the law or he was not at all afraid of it.

Perhaps both.

"Got someone else exiting the building," I said. "Second security guard went inside. They're probably going to move Goddard out through the back."

"You got the vantage point." Jack paused as a loud truck drove past. "Think we should follow him or stick to Goddard?"

I looked between the building and the retreating figure. Knowing who the new guy was would be handy, but the primary target was still Goddard. Intel from other sources was great. We liked to do our own scouting ahead of an op though. Less room for things to go wrong, and when they did, at least we were prepared for every scenario.

"Let's stick to Goddard," I said. "But this new guy is heading your way." I gave him a quick description of the man. "Take some photos so we can ID him later. We'll fall back for now so Goddard's team isn't as spooked come lunchtime when we scope out the restaurant."

The rest of the day was uneventful in comparison to the morning. Goddard had another meeting at lunch, this one lasting twice as long as the first. Jack and I decided to keep our distance. There was no point in risking exposure again. We knew where he'd end his evening.

But that didn't mean there were no surprises waiting for us when Goddard arrived. We took up a spot across the street in a quiet café. We ordered coffee and sat deep enough inside that we wouldn't be spotted. Two of Goddard's men were stationed out front, same as earlier. The third was presumably on the other side of the building.

But this time we knew one of the people with Goddard.

Jack leaned forward. "Well I'll be damned."

"Is that your girlfriend from the beach?" I asked.

Goddard had just exited his car and extended a hand to the woman who emerged after him. She wore a sleek black dress and had her hair pinned back in curls.

"What the hell is she doing here?" Jack said.

"Beats me," I said. "What'd you say her name was?"

"Michelle." Jack lifted his coffee to his lips. His eyes never wavered.

"Call her."

"Now?"

I nodded and passed him my phone. "See how she reacts."

He dialed the number and put the call on speaker. Michelle placed her hand on Goddard's shoulder as she reached into her purse and pulled out her cell. She smiled and Goddard nodded, heading inside without her. Michelle walked a couple dozen feet down the sidewalk and answered.

"Hello?"

"Hey, it's Jack."

"From the beach this morning." Her voice was light, her accent a little heavier than Javier's. I could hear the smile in her voice, but she was checking her watch and looking back over her shoulder.

"I was wondering if you'd like to grab a drink tonight?"

"Oh." Her shoulders hunched up, tensed. "I can't tonight, I'm sorry. What about tomorrow?"

Jack looked over at me and I nodded.

"Tomorrow works."

"Great." There was a genuine smile on her face now. "I'll see you then. And Jack?"

"Yeah?"

"I'm glad you called."

"Me too."

We both watched as Michelle hung up the phone and shoved it back in her purse before smoothing her hair and making her way back inside. She disappeared into the dark interior of the restaurant.

I HUNG UP THE PHONE WITH FRANK WITH MORE FORCE THAN was necessary. I hated talking to that guy, and I knew the feeling was mutual. Still, the information he gave me seemed solid, as little of it as there was.

I picked up the surveillance photos from last night and the ones I took today. Jack was out with the girl from the beach, so it was my job to go over what we already knew. It wasn't much. Hopefully it would be enough to get the job done.

The man from the other morning was named Vasquez, according to Frank. He was a former police officer who had ended up in Costa Rica and found himself on the other side of the law. He stayed in the shadows and didn't cause too much trouble, so Frank and other intelligence agency leaders weren't hung up on bringing him in just yet. For now it worked better for them to see who he was meeting with and bring down the people he was working for.

Frank didn't have anything on the girl and no one else Goddard had met with in the last two days caused Frank any concern. He told me to get the job done and phone it in when we were on our way out of the country. He hadn't made any improvements in his bedside manner over the years.

By the time Jack walked through the door, I had a solid plan of attack. I filled him in on Vasquez, the lack of information on Michelle, and which building I thought would be our best shot at taking out Goddard.

"So who's taking the shot?" Jack asked.

"Flip for it?" I pulled a quarter out of my pocket.

"Tails never fails," he said.

I flipped the coin and let it land on the table with a clatter. "Heads."

"I'll be on the ground then."

"Probably for the best," I said, "considering they already spotted me once."

He nodded. "I've got another date with Michelle. I'll head there directly following the shot and you can crash our little party twenty minutes in."

"I'm sure she'll appreciate that."

He laughed. "As long as you don't stay too long."

"Depends on how good the food is," I said. "And the company."

"You looking to get yourself into trouble, big man?"

It was my turn to laugh this time. "If this night goes according to plan, I might need a little trouble to keep it interesting."

CHAPTER SIX

J ack walked past the restaurant, staring down at a map he
didn't need. A brief rainstorm had left the sidewalk slick.
Puddles formed where the ground had sunk over time. It
smelled of motor oil and garbage and grill smoke. Groups of
people passed by him, paying no attention to the killer stalking the
streets.

Goddard hadn't showed up yet, but they knew it would only be a
couple of minutes until he showed his face. Goddard's routine was as
rigid as his demeanor. That made him predictable. And they loved a
predictable target.

"In position." Bear's voice came through Jack's earpiece. "How's
it look down there?"

"Busy tonight," Jack said. "Lots of people on the street. Let's hope
it clears out later."

"Copy," Bear said. "Let me know if you spot anything out of the
ordinary."

Before Jack could respond, he felt a light tap on his shoulder
followed by a hint of jasmine. "Jack?"

He turned at the touch. "Michelle? I thought we were meeting later?"

"I could say the same." She raised an eyebrow. The neon lights from a shop sign reflected in her dark eyes. "But something came up. I'll call you later?"

"Sure." He watched as she gave him a sad smile and walked across the street into the restaurant.

"So much for avoiding trouble," Bear said.

"You're the one who wanted to keep it interesting." Jack paused a beat. "You got eyes on what's going on in there?"

"She just hugged Goddard. Looks like they're grabbing a table in the back. Ah, yup. They're out of view now."

Jack walked further down the street and found a bench under a blown-out lamp post. "Something doesn't feel right."

"You mean because the woman who gave you her number seemingly at random has now met with our target twice in the same number of days?"

"You want to pull back?" Jack asked.

"Op's not lost yet."

"I could get inside. Take an up-close shot."

"You'll be spotted by everyone in there if you try that," Bear said. "Not worth it. You get inside and direct traffic. Get him out of there. Besides, I'm the better shot."

"You wish." Jack stood up and crossed the street to the restaurant.

"Don't get too close. I've already been spotted. We don't need you on their radar, too."

"Roger that."

He walked through the door and up to hostess at the entrance. The younger woman was thin, dark-haired, full-lipped. She looked him up and down then past him. He must not have met her criteria.

"Bar open?" He pointed behind her to the long countertop with a dozen or so stools.

"Sure is," she said. "Go on back."

He nodded and dropped the smile once he passed her.

Jack approached the bar and found a seat that allowed him to use the mirror to look directly behind him at Goddard's table. He ordered a beer and watched the scene unfold as he waited.

Michelle was just one of several people sitting at the table with Goddard, laughing, drinking, and having a good time. They were the loudest group in the restaurant, but no one seemed to mind. And those that did got up and left quietly. He tried to take in all the faces, but his gaze kept going back to hers.

About thirty minutes and two beers into his time at the bar, a woman slid her way between Jack and the stool next to him. When he looked over, he first saw the low cut of her dress and the red stone necklace that lay in the center of her cleavage. As his gaze traveled upward, he saw Michelle smiling at him.

"Hi," she said.

"Hey." Jack lifted his beer to his mouth before realizing it was empty. He signaled the waiter for another. This one he'd nurse. It was for show only.

"You following me, Jack?"

"I thought I'd get that drink after all." He looked past her and over his shoulder at the table where Goddard sat. "Am I bothering you?"

"Not so much," she said. "But you don't look like you're having a very good time over here by yourself."

He shrugged. "I had a date with a beautiful woman. Turns out she stood me up for an older man."

Michelle laughed. It was light and breathy. "Senator Goddard is a married man."

"That doesn't stop them." He nodded his head in acknowledgment as the bartender placed another beer in front of him. "Senator?"

Michelle nodded. "Would you like to meet him?"

"Bad idea," Bear whispered in Jack's ear.

"I doubt a senator would want to meet a guy like me."

"Nonsense. Another American in Costa Rica? He'll be delighted."

He opened his mouth to argue, but she hooked her arm around his elbow and started to drag him over to the table. He barely had time to grab his drink before she introduced him to the senator. He heard Bear groan on the other end of his earpiece.

"Senator," Michelle said, touching his shoulder gently. He instantly turned toward her. "Senator, I'd like you to meet a friend of mine. This is Jack."

Jack stuck out a hand while the senator stood. They shook briefly. "It's a pleasure to meet you, sir."

"You too, Jack," the senator said. He had a politician's smile plastered across his face. "Any friend of Ms. Hernandez's is a friend of mine. Please, sit."

"No, I don't want to inconvenience you guys." An untouched steak caught his eye.

"I insist," Goddard said. "Jordan, bring up another chair for our new guest."

A squirrelly young man with severely parted hair jumped up and grabbed a seat for Jack. He placed it next to Michelle's and the two of them squeezed in and joined the rowdy table.

Goddard leaned forward and spoke directly to him. The rest of the table seemed to be wrapped up in their own conversations. No one was paying much attention, except for Jordan.

"How did you two meet?" Goddard asked.

Jack opened his mouth to answer, but Michelle beat him to the punch. "College. Jack went out with my roommate for a few months, but it was bound to fail." Her lie was smooth and she laughed easily. "Jack and I became friends, but I hadn't heard from him in years. Can you imagine running into him here, of all places?"

Her adeptness at lying was not lost on Jack.

"What are the chances?" Goddard said. He took a deep sip of wine. "Which college?"

"Pardon?" Jack asked, leaning forward as if he didn't hear the question in order to give him more time to come up with an answer.

Goddard wagged his index finger between both of them. "Which college did you two attend together?"

Jack looked to Michelle to see if she was going to continue the lie, but she only looked back at him with wide eyes, waiting to see what he'd come up with.

"Michigan," Jack said. He heard Bear chuckle in his ear. It was a partial lie. He'd declared to attend, but then opted for the Marines after high school. "I didn't last long there, unfortunately. Probably part of the reason why Tina and I didn't make it. Had trouble with school, but did decent in sports. That only carried me so far, though."

"Go Blue," Bear whispered in his ear.

"Go Blue," Jack repeated.

Michelle and Goddard both laughed, and Jack felt her hand snake across his knee and give it a squeeze. If he hadn't felt like he was walking into a trap before, he certainly did now. What was Michelle up to, and why did she need to lie to Goddard about how they knew each other?

The rest of dinner passed by in a blur. Goddard mostly ignored Jack, talking to several of his guests in turn. He seemed pretty buzzed by the end, but he was ever the politician, leaning in whenever someone wanted his ear and then nodding and smiling at whatever they said. His assistant made sure he had plenty of wine, but when it hit eleven on the dot, he lightly tapped on his boss' shoulder and gave him a nod.

Goddard's guests stood and began dissipating in twos and threes. The senator placed an arm around Michelle's shoulders and shook Jack's hand again, this time extending the grip in his intoxicated state.

"Jack, Jack," Goddard said. "The night is young. You should join us at Vita's."

"Vita's?" he asked, looking between the senator and Michelle. He couldn't quite read the expression on his old friend's face.

"A bar owned by a friend of mine," Goddard said. "Come. Join us. I promise, you won't regret it."

"Wanna bet," Bear said.

"All right." Presumably the bar would be a little more low-key. If Bear couldn't get a shot off while they were loading into the cars, Jack would be able to do it at the next spot. "Why not?"

"Wonderful," Michelle said. "But first I need to use the ladies' room."

"Jordan," Goddard called over his shoulder. "Call Santiago and tell him we're coming."

"Yes, sir." Jordan put a phone to his ear.

Jack felt a buzzing in his pocket and pulled out his own phone. It was Javier's burner line. This close to the hit, there could only be one reason why he'd be calling.

"Excuse me," Jack said to Goddard, taking a step away from the table. "I have to grab this real quick."

"No problem." Goddard turned back to Jordan to check on their reservations.

Jack held the phone to his ear. "Hello?"

"You have to call it off." It was Javier. His voice was tight and terse and had a tinge of panic to it.

"What?"

"You have to call it off!" he shouted.

"Slow down, man." Jack turned away from the senator and cupping his other hand over the phone. "What's going on?"

"They have my daughter," Javier said. "They have my daughter and they'll kill her if anything happens to the senator. You must call it off. Now."

Before Jack could ask for specifics, he noticed Michelle step out of the bathroom and level an icy stare at him. The light and playful woman from the table was gone. He raised an eyebrow at her, and she pointedly looked over his shoulder and toward the front entrance.

He turned and saw Goddard speaking with the hostess, one hand congenially on her arm and the other pressing open the door. Things started to move in slow motion.

"Jack, do you hear me? Call it off now!"

With the phone still held to his ear, he could think of only one thing to say.

"Shit."

CHAPTER SEVEN

I heard Jack swear under his breath as a crack of light spilling out onto the sidewalk drew all my attention. It was Goddard and in a few seconds he'd be in my sights.

"He's got one foot out. I'm lined up. Two more steps and he's dead."

"Don't do it," Jack said.

I heard a woman say, "What?" at the same time I did. The static in the earpiece went silent. Jack had terminated the connection. A beat passed and I saw my cell light up at my feet. I was on the rooftop across the street, my aim perfect and my window closing. I could take the shot or I could answer the cell. I couldn't do both.

But Jack had called it off. I grabbed the phone and cradled it between my shoulder and my ear. When I looked back through the scope, Goddard was already halfway in the black sedan.

"What?"

"Javier's pulling us back," Jack said on the other end.

I saw Michelle step through the door. Her face was drawn tight. She looked confused or angry. She threw a glance over her shoulder, presumably at Jack, and continued onward and into Goddard's car.

"Why?" I asked.

"Cartel has his daughter." Jack's voice was low and close to the mic on the phone. "If this goes down, they'll send him her head."

"Shit."

"Exactly." He ended the call.

I watched for a moment longer as Jack exited the bar and flagged Goddard's sedan before it could pull away. I broke down my gear and heard snippets of Jack's conversation with the senator rising and falling with the breeze. He was getting out of meeting up at the second spot. Something about an emergency call from a friend. After the vehicle pulled away, Jack restored the connection to his comms unit.

With precision and a bead of sweat rolling down my temple, I broke the rifle down and placed it in my bag and swung it over my shoulder. Staying low, I crept toward the door that would lead to the stairway that led down to the first floor. I was on top of an apartment building, one of the few in this part of town. It was a classy neighborhood, but the age of the brick façade made it look as worn down as it did historic.

The trip to ground level was a quick one, and I met no one on my way through. The stairwell smelled of bleach. My steps echoed throughout. Once I hit the last step, I slid through the back door and checked the alley up and down. The same vagabond was still sleeping on a trio of cardboard boxes surrounded by his belongings. Maybe he was the reason for the bleach. He clutched a half-eaten burger. If it weren't for the occasional snore, I would have thought he were dead.

I headed off in the opposite direction, shoving my hands in my pockets and keeping my head low. I couldn't exactly make myself look smaller, but walking with an air of determination usually made people's eyes slide right past you.

The street was still busy by the time I reached the main thoroughfare. Lines stretched out of the entrances to bars and restaurants. The smell of local cuisine drifted through the opened doors. My mouth watered. I could hear the crowd all around me and in the piece in my ear. Jack and I were waiting to discuss everything when we met at our rendezvous point, but we weren't about to cut communication completely. This complication with Javier's daughter put an unknown element into the mix. If someone had her, did that mean they knew about the op? Did they know about us? My mind raced, thinking of who might've sold us out.

"You're the one that wanted to keep it interesting tonight." Jack was leaning against the corner of a building, looking up at the light-washed sky. He appeared relaxed, but I could sense the tension rolling off him. He didn't like the situation any more than I did.

I ignored the jab and placed my hand on the cool brick next to his head. "What in the hell is going on?"

"I don't know, man."

He pushed off the building and we made our way through the crowd. It thinned out a couple streets over where there were more shops and offices than restaurants. The road we had parked the Land Rover on was practically dead.

I scanned the street before sliding in behind the wheel. The stiff leather squeaked as I eased down. I spotted a couple teens smoking across the street, that was it. We sat in silence for a minute, trying to process the sequence of events that had occurred in the last hour or so.

I gripped the wheel until my knuckles turned white. "Walk me through it."

Jack knew I had heard everything he had while he was on the inside, but having him paint a visual changed the whole situation. He rolled the window down and stuck his arm outside. A cool breeze finally dried the sweat on my forehead.

"After she spotted me, I went to the bar and had a couple drinks. She came up to me thirty minutes later, invited me to the table. She acted just how she had the last couple times I saw her, but she's a good liar, man. No tells. No hesitations."

"Trained?"

"I don't know. Could be natural." Jack rolled the window up and nodded toward the ignition. I started up the car and pulled away from the curb before he continued. "Could be a criminal. She's got this...air about her."

"An air?"

"Yeah, an air." He shifted in his seat. He was visibly frustrated. "Dangerous. I thought it was just her personality. Hotheaded. Stubborn. She's got an attitude."

"Just the way you like 'em."

He ignored me. "But there's something else. The way she carries herself. She's not afraid. Not of me, that's for sure."

"She might feel protected by Goddard."

"It's more than that. She played him so smoothly. She didn't even blink an eye. She either had that story ready or she's just that good."

"And if she had the story ready—"

"Then she knows I'm not who I say I am."

I eased off the gas and took a sharp right, checking my rearview for any tails. The road had been clear so far, and it appeared to remain that way. "Think she knows exactly who you are?"

Jack watched the blur of buildings whiz by for a moment before he answered. "I don't know. She had this look on her face right before she left that said, 'Don't screw this up.'"

"So she knows why you were there?"

"Goddard is a high profile American politician. He probably gets death threats all the time. She could know I was trying to get close to him without knowing who sent us."

I nodded a couple times. "Think she knew who you were that day on the beach? I mean, maybe she's been watching us since we landed."

"Hell if I know." Jack ran a hand through his hair. "If she did, she's one damn good actress."

"It happens to the best of us." My stomach rumbled loud enough to draw his attention.

"I don't like being played, man."

"Me neither." I pressed the gas pedal down a little further. "So let's go get some answers."

CHAPTER EIGHT

I t was late by the time we pulled up to the concrete building. The jungle roared with the sound of the night. It's inhabitants were out in full force. The air was crisp, free of the trappings of the city.

Javier was already waiting for us, his agitation mostly hidden by years of training. But no amount of training prepared you for the sickening feeling of knowing someone you loved was in serious danger. The kind of people we dealt with didn't give second chances, even for little girls who had nothing to do with their father's job.

Our second trip to the facility had a different feel to it than the first. Javier scanned the trees once, quickly, and then walked inside, barely waiting for us to keep up. His secretary was not sitting at her desk and everything seemed to be shut down for the night. There wasn't a night assistant at the desk.

Javier was halfway down the stairs before Jack had hit the first step, with me close behind. He threw a glance at me over his shoulder but there was nothing to say. He was all business right now and as much as we didn't know about him or his daughter, this was our op that went sideways. She didn't deserve to be mixed up in any of this. I couldn't blame the man for wanting to put this experience behind him and just find his daughter.

Javier stopped several doors ahead of his office and entered a long room that housed only a single table and four chairs. He stepped to the side until we had walked in, and then he shut the door behind us. He stood there with his arms across his chest, eying us warily.

Jack was the first to speak. "An interrogation room?" There was a slight challenge in his voice.

"Who did you talk to about the op?" Javier took two steps forward and put his hands on his hips. In any other situation, I would've gone toe to toe with him, encouraging him to take the first swing. But this wasn't the time or the place.

I pulled out a chair and sat down, arms crossed over my chest, left ankle over my right knee. I stared up at him with as transparent a face as I could pull off. "Frank's the only one we've talked to."

"He wouldn't betray me."

Jack followed my lead and sat down in the chair next to mine. He kicked one leg up on the table. "You're one of the lucky few, then."

"Who else?" Javier leaned forward on the table, but he was no longer hostile. He was desperate. Lines of sweat stretched from his sideburns to the corner of his jaw.

"The only other person we had contact with was a guy name Thorne," I said. "One of Skinner's guys. We don't know him. Could be he didn't even look at the dossier."

"Nosy little shit probably opened it the second Frank was out of sight," Jack said.

I scratched at my chin. "Possible. Can't vouch for him, but if you trust Frank, then you can probably trust Thorne."

Jack scoffed but he didn't say anything else.

Javier nodded his head a few times. His eyes went glassy as he presumably thought through his own contacts. "I will reach out to Frank, but I think it's a dead end."

"Our aliases are clean," Jack said. "We didn't have any trouble on the way here. If someone knows what we're doing here, it must be from your end."

Javier stiffened, but I held up a hand and shot Jack a look. "He means here in Costa Rica. Someone either got here ahead of us or found out once we started tailing Goddard."

"Were you spotted?"

Jack and I exchanged a look. Javier struck the table with his fist and stalked to the other end of the room where he put his head against the wall. I could hear him taking deep breaths to calm himself down.

"It happens, man," I said. "And I'm sorry it had to happen on this op. But someone would have to recognize me, and then connect me to you, and then find your daughter and have the means of taking her. That narrows the list. I don't think we're looking at someone coming after us. This is a pretty big warning sign for you."

"How do you know she was taken?" Jack asked.

Javier pushed away from the wall and sat down opposite me. He pulled his phone out of his pocket. "This came to my personal cell from her number."

I slid the phone over and placed it between me and Jack. A video took up the whole screen. I hit the white triangle in the middle and it immediately began to play.

A girl about nine or ten was sitting in a chair, her hands tied behind her back and a white strip of cloth in her mouth, gagging her. The cloth was tinged red in a few spots. She filled most of the frame, but I could see a stack of boxes in the background and a high window near the left-hand corner of the screen.

A hand reached over and pulled the gag from her mouth. The girl flinched, but she didn't cry out. Instead, she looked up at her captor and pleaded with him, tears streaming down her face. Blood trickled from her nose.

"Speak," a voice said, its accent thick. Hispanic. Male. Could be a native or anyone from the surrounding countries. Javier and Jack would have a better ear for the accent than I would.

The girl turned to the camera. The hidden side of her face now revealed a large bruise.

"Daddy," she said. "Daddy, please."

"Say it," her captor shouted, and this time the girl did flinch.

"Daddy, they say you have to leave the senator alone. They say if you don't—" she hiccuped here and fresh tears started down her face "—then they'll deliver me to you in pieces." Her voice wobbled along with her chin, but she bit her lip and looked directly into the camera. "If you leave him alone, they'll give you an address in three days."

The camera tilted to the side and the screen went black. When I looked up at Javier, his jaw was clenched so tightly I thought his teeth would crack.

Jack leaned forward and with a soft voice, asked, "What's her name?"

Javier took three deep breaths in through his nose to control his voice before speaking. "Camila."

"Did they send anything else?" I asked.

Javier shook his head.

"They're in a warehouse of some sort," Jack said. "Something about it, looked dank, wet. Maybe by the sea. I could be way off on that."

"I've got my men combing through every pixel." He looked up at me. "They'll find something."

He sounded as though he was trying to convince himself more than us.

"And when they do," I said, "we'll track her down and take out every single one of those bastards."

Javier nodded and was silent for a moment. His gaze drifted down to the table.

Jack and I exchanged a look. I made to stand up. "We've got a couple channels I can reach out to. They'll start doing some ground-work. Maybe turn something up we can use."

Javier stood up as well. The look on his face said there was something else left unsaid.

I eyed him warily. I trusted Javier, probably more than I should considering how long we'd known the guy. But he was in a desperate situation now. If the kidnappers demanded Jack's head or mine, I had no doubt Javier would serve them up on a silver platter to get his daughter back. And I couldn't even hold that against him.

Before the man could say anything else, the door burst open and a woman stepped through. Jack and I whipped our heads around. Javier stood staring straight ahead as if he knew this inevitability had only been seconds away from becoming reality.

Standing there in the room with us, seething, was none other than the woman from the beach. Michelle. She looked different outside of her slinky dresses and curled hair, but there was no doubt as to who it was. Her tactical boots, dark cargo pants, tight shirt, and a light jacket made her look as different as possible from the seductress she had been before.

The scowl on her face, which was aimed directly at Jack, did wonders to make it look like she could take out all three of us without breaking a sweat.

"Gentleman, this is Sadie." Javier finally turned toward the new addition to the room, but he didn't quite meet her eyes. "She's CIA."

CHAPTER NINE

Jack's chair screeched on the floor as he lurched up. "What the hell are you doing here?"

"I could ask you the same thing." Michelle—*Sadie*—stared as though she were trying to set him on fire. "Someone better have some goddamn answers for me."

I noticed her accent was gone, her voice a little huskier. She wasn't trying to put on a front now. This was pure, unfiltered Sadie. I learned a long time ago to never underestimate any woman, and Sadie seemed about as formidable as they came. It was apparent that Jack wasn't concerned about staying in her good graces, however.

He walked around me and squared off with the woman he had been cozying up to only hours earlier. "We don't owe you shit."

Sadie turned her back on Jack. The dismissal ate at him. "I was told you had been informed of my presence."

Javier pinched the bridge of his nose. "It seems I did not receive all the relevant information. Your handler purposefully misdirected me."

"We're the CIA," Sadie said. "You should know better than to expect straight answers from us. You knew what you needed to know."

"Obviously not," Javier said. I was struck by the calm in his voice. It felt more dangerous than if he had been yelling as loudly as the woman. "We were never informed of your relationship with Goddard."

Sadie opened her mouth to retort, but I stepped forward and attempted to intervene. "Can we start at the beginning? As interesting as it is to watch you two trade verbal blows, it's not helping anyone."

Javier took a deep breath and sat back down, crossing one leg over the other and feigning as much relaxation as he could. I followed suit, and after a moment Sadie joined us at the table. I eyed Jack, waiting for him to give in, but he leaned up against the wall with his arms crossed, never taking his gaze off her. She ignored him.

I turned to Sadie and as flatly as I could, asked, "What business do you have with Goddard?"

She scoffed. "You can't expect me to give two strangers that kind of information."

"But we're not strangers, are we?" I leaned forward across the table, careful to keep my voice neutral. "You already know who we are."

Sadie paused for a moment, glancing between me and Jack. "Jack Noble and Riley Logan. You two don't exactly keep a low profile."

I chuckled, but Jack didn't seem as amused. I stifled my laughter and turned to Javier. "Did you inform her?"

"He didn't need to. The moment I spotted him," she pointed at Jack without ever taking her eyes off me, "I knew who he was. We've met before, Jack. Briefly. I wasn't surprised you didn't recognize me. You were pretty wasted."

I jumped in before Jack could respond. "So you knew why we were in town?"

"No." She shifted in her seat, stretching her arms out in front of her. "I figured it was for something clandestine, but I didn't think it had anything to do with my op."

"And what is your op exactly?" Jack asked.

Sadie raised an eyebrow, but said nothing.

"Tell them," Javier said. His voice was still quiet, low.

"I don't owe them an explanation—"

Javier finally erupted. "But someone owes me one!" He turned to her and leaned forward. It was the first time Sadie had shown any shock or discomfort. "They have my daughter, and so help me God, if you do not unfuck this situation, I will find a way to make sure you are held responsible."

"I-I didn't know." Sadie looked at me, and I nodded. Her face softened. "I'm sorry, Javier. I didn't know."

"All of this could have been avoided if everyone had just been straight with me to begin with." He took a deep breath and leaned back in his chair again, his eyes closed and his lips pursed. "Tell us what you know so I can find my daughter. She's only ten for God's sake. She knows nothing about my life. She does not deserve that kind of burden."

"I have to check in with my handler." Sadie shifted uncomfortably. "I can't just—"

"You can and you will." Jack's voice matched Javier's now. He didn't say it with an explicit amount of authority, but the warning was there. "Show her the video."

Javier blew out a breath and pushed his phone in front of her. He stood up as soon as she pushed play and walked across the room, as if trying to get as far away from his problem as possible. But Camila's cries bounced around the room as if the walls amplified them. I could practically hear Javier grinding his teeth.

Sadie pushed the phone away from her and inhaled sharply. There were no tears in her eyes, but it was obvious the video had affected her. She bobbed her head up and down a few times before she looked up at each one of us in turn, her eyes finally settling on Javier, who had returned to stand in the middle of the room.

"You weren't purposefully misinformed, Javier. At least not at first."

"Excuses won't get you anywhere," Jack said.

Sadie pierced him with a look. "Neither will interruptions. Look, I get you like us about as much as we like you, but we're on the same side here. We never intended for anyone to get hurt, let alone a ten-year-old girl. We had to play our cards close to the chest. This turned into something much bigger than we initially thought it would."

"Explain." Javier looked like a man near the end of his rope.

Sadie took a deep breath. "We initially had our sight set on Mateo Martinez, the leader of a drug cartel. He's smart. He's been at this for a while. He knows how to stay off the radar. We were never too concerned with him because there was always someone bigger to go after. But he's been subtly expanding for years and out of nowhere he's behind as many legitimate operations as he is illegal ones."

"Harder to take down a guy if he's got that many legal fronts keeping his business afloat," I said.

"Exactly." Sadie drummed her fingers against the desk for a moment before she continued. "They set me up inside one of Martinez's legitimate businesses. I posed as an accountant. Played my hand right so I could show him how useful I could be to the other side of his empire."

"How long did that take?"

"Three years. Couple close calls. But once I was in, I had all access. Saved the bastards a lot of money, allowed a lot of people to get hurt in the process."

"That's the game," Jack said. He sounded calmer, but his voice was still apathetic. "I bet you helped more people than you hurt."

Sadie shook her head. "Game's not over yet. The day we were planning to take the compound, someone unexpected walked through the door."

"Goddard," I said.

She nodded. "Recognized him instantly. We thought he had been tricked at first. Thought he was in danger and that we'd have to save his sorry ass."

"Surprise."

Sadie laughed, but there was no humor behind it. "He walked around like he owned the place, and that's when we realized he did. Martinez doesn't take orders from anyone, but Goddard put him in his place pretty damn quickly."

"Does the senator have something on him?"

"I think it's just a good business deal. Goddard is good for business, and Martinez is always looking to expand. Ever since Goddard came on board, Martinez's profits have tripled."

"And now you want to nail Goddard and hope you can take Martinez down at the same time," Jack said.

"We're days away from busting him and then you idiots walk through the door."

"Technically, Jack walked through the door." I smiled. "I was on the roof."

"And you almost screwed up the whole thing."

"You're not the only one trying to do your job," Jack said. "Don't come at us like we're doing something wrong here."

Sadie swiveled around to face him. "Goddard should go to jail, not get a bullet in the head."

"Says who?" Jack shook his head. "Imagine the scandal back home when everything comes out about him."

"And an assassinated senator is less messy than a corrupt one?" she said.

"Sometimes, yeah." Jack was getting visibly agitated again. "You have to think about the long con."

Sadie laughed. "Only criminals think about the long con."

I silenced Jack with a look and turned to Javier. "This is about more than just Goddard now. We'll help you get your daughter back."

Javier nodded gravely.

"Of course." Sadie laid a hand on his shoulder. "We'll do whatever it takes to get her back."

I saw Sadie's eyes shift. "But?"

She removed her hand from Javier's arm. "But once we get her back, nothing changes. The op is mine. I've spent too many years setting this up just to watch someone else take it from me."

"And what the hell are we supposed to do about our op?"

"Not my problem."

I heard Jack's phone buzzing, and as he picked it up, a grin spread across his face. "It's about to become your problem. Hey, Frank."

The smile immediately vanished from his face. He went to say something else, but Frank must've cut him off. Jack snapped his mouth shut, and after another minute, he pocketed his phone without saying anything more.

"He calling us off?" I didn't like the idea of giving up an op we'd already spent time on, but my mind kept going back to that little girl. If we got her out of there in one piece, my conscience would be clear.

"Even better." Jack's gaze slid over to Sadie. "He wants us to work with the CIA."

"Over my dead body." She pulled out her phone. "I'm calling my handler right now."

Before Sadie could push a single button, her phone lit up. I didn't catch the number on the screen before she held it to her ear. The conversation played out almost the same as the one between Jack and Frank.

When Sadie threw her phone down on the table and didn't say anymore, we all knew what it meant.

"Now that the pissing match is over," Javier said, a new determination on his face, "we can get started on bringing home my Camila."

CHAPTER TEN

The four of us gathered in a different room closer to Javier's office. It felt less like an interrogation room and more like it was meant as headquarters ahead of a mission. And that's exactly what we were treating it as—regardless of if we agreed over whether it was a good idea.

I sat down in the chair closest to the vent. A stream of cold air that smelled like stale chips hit me in the face. It had been a long day, and I was comfortable, so I ignored the odor. "We got a plan?"

Sadie had been quiet since her phone call. "Our first priority is Camila. Once we get her, we move in to take down Goddard."

I felt as though I was walking across a frozen lake that was cracking underneath me with every passing second. "And how are we going to handle that?"

Sadie worked her jaw before speaking between clenched teeth. "It seems as though your boss won the argument on that one. The plan is elimination."

Jack had the wherewithal not to look too cocky. He just nodded his head and let his gaze meet mine for a fraction of a second.

Sadie continued. "And with that, we'll lose God knows how much intelligence."

"We still don't know who has my Camila." Javier spread a map out in front of them. His voice was steady, but the look in his eye said he was barely holding back the hopelessness. "The video indicates she's being kept in a warehouse. I've circled the known locations of Martinez's buildings, all of which store either weapons or drugs."

Jack leaned on the table and scanned the map. "There has to be a couple dozen here."

Javier nodded. "We must narrow it down. If we start looking for her in every building, someone will catch on."

"Reach out to your contacts," Sadie said. "Do you know her last known location? Where do you live? Is it somewhere that CCTV is prominent? Surely you know people with access to the local network. If we can find out who took her, it'll help us pinpoint her location. Then it's just a matter of finding the safest way to retrieve her."

Javier nodded, stood, then left the room. An uncomfortable silence took his place.

Sadie turned back to the maps. She worked her right thumb and middle finger on her temples. "I have a meeting with Goddard tomorrow. You two can sit tight until I get the lay of the land."

Jack moved into her field of view and crossed his arms. "Who said you're calling the shots?"

"I did."

"Your boss seems to be answering to someone else."

Sadie rolled her shoulders. I could feel her anger clawing to get out, but she pushed it back with several deep breaths. "Look, I know we got off on the wrong foot, but we're both here for the same reason. Can't we work together?"

"You don't want us to work together," he said. "You want us sitting on the sidelines. We're not those guys. We get more done when we're on the field."

"He's got a point," I said. "We can help you."

She lowered her head. "You're a liability."

Jack sat down, diffusing some of the tension in the room. "We're trained. Bear's a good shot and I'm relentless. Goddard likes me. You saw that yourself. We can use that to our advantage."

"He doesn't take to people easily. What you saw earlier isn't him. He was relaxed because he wanted to be. That, and he had plenty of security there. Next time he sees you, you'll be tested."

"It won't be anything I haven't been through before."

Sadie laughed. "You don't know him."

"And you don't know me." Jack held up his hands before she could snap out a retort. "All I'm saying is give me a chance."

"Giving you a chance could cause this whole thing to blow up in our faces."

Jack leaned forward. "Not giving me a chance could do worse."

She sighed. "Fine. But I've got to call the shots on this one."

I stepped in to mediate. "That's fine. We work on this together, but we defer to you. You've been in there longer. We're not here to blow your cover. We just want to get the job done."

Jack paused a moment before nodding. It wasn't easy to give up control on our op, but the game had changed. It wasn't our asses on the line anymore. We had to play this the right way.

"Deal." Sadie sunk into her chair, let out an exhausted sigh.

I gave her a moment before I spoke again. "Tell us about this meeting tomorrow."

"Right." She sat up again, forcing energy back into her body. "There seems to be an issue with Martinez. I'm not sure what's going on yet, but Goddard is looking to have him audited, so to speak. He wants me to check out the books."

"Is this an unusual request from him?"

She nodded. "He's usually pretty hands off. Goddard is a good businessman, but he's a big picture kind of guy. He has other people worry about the day-to-day issues. If he's stepping in himself to check on Martinez, there must be something larger at work."

"Any idea what it could be?" Jack asked.

"There are always rumors, but they usually don't hold water."

"What's the strongest one?" I asked.

Sadie's eyes unfocused, moving from left to right as if she were reading invisible notes in the air in front of her. "His nephew has been moving up in the ranks. People listen to him, but he's an idiot. He doesn't have his uncle's tactical brain. He leads through fear and intimidation."

"That can get you far in this world," I said.

"Not with Goddard. He respects Martinez because he takes the slow and steady route. Less chance for failure. It took both of them a long time to get to where they are, but they did it through their guile, not through intimidation."

"So we're looking at a possible coup?" Jack said. "Where do we fit into all of this?"

Sadie formed her words slowly. "My recommendation can get you through the door. He's met you already, Jack, so he might be more open to a collaboration."

"What kind of collaboration?"

"Your story doesn't have to be far from the truth. Former military turned independent contractor. You're in town for another job, willing to pick up another for the right price. We promise that you're discreet. You're even willing to offer a discount since you owe me a favor."

"Do I?"

"If we have a business history, it'll go over well," Sadie said. "I can tell him I didn't bring it up right away because it had been several years since we'd seen each other and I didn't know you were still in the business."

"Seems plausible enough." I tapped my fingers impatiently on the rough surface of the table. Jack and I were men of action. Sitting around going through every step of the plan, however necessary, was tedious. "There are a lot of places where this could go sideways, though."

"I don't disagree with you." She paused, bit the corner of her bottom lip. "But we're throwing this together last minute. It's not going to be perfect. Experience will be a big factor here, gents."

"What about the big man?" Jack jabbed a thumb in my direction.

I turned toward her.

She nodded at me for a moment before saying, "Backup. We'll need you out there in case this thing goes off the rails. You'll have to be our cover in the event we need to get out of there quickly."

"Probably best I hang back anyway. Goddard's security guys didn't like the look of me the first time they saw me. I doubt they'd like me any better the second time."

"So what now?" Jack shifted in his chair. He was getting as impatient as I was.

"Now, we get some rest." Sadie stood up and crossed the room and placed one hand on the doorknob. "In the morning, I'll call Goddard."

CHAPTER ELEVEN

March 26, 2006

Goddard hung up the phone and rubbed his hand along his jaw. He rarely shaved when in country, and this trip was no exception. The bristles on his face scratched at his soft fingertips. He'd been an avid guitar player when he was younger and had thick callouses on his fingertips. Those days were long past. The only strings he played were the ones attached to those he had control over.

The smell of his untouched breakfast lingered in the air. There was too much on his mind to eat this morning. A problem had finally reached its peak and now it was time to deal with it.

"Sir?" Jordan asked.

Goddard looked up. He had forgotten his assistant was still in the room. That seemed to be the man's specialty—disappearing into the background when he wasn't needed and reappearing immediately without prompting at the perfect moment. Jordan's hand was hovering over his PDA, waiting for instruction.

"That was Michelle. She had a recommendation."

"Jack?"

Goddard tipped his head in his assistant's direction, said nothing.

"Her reason?"

Normally Goddard would remind anyone who pried into his business where exactly they stood in relation to him—which was to say as far away from having the privilege of being able to ask such questions. Jordan was the exception, however. The man had become an extension of Goddard and had earned his right to ask. Life was easier when he was as informed as Goddard.

"It seems she thinks Jack can help us with our Mateo Martinez problem. He's an independent contractor." Goddard raised an eyebrow and the assistant nodded in understanding. "She promised he can be discreet."

Jordan tapped on his device before looking back up at the senator. "Michelle has proven her loyalty many times over."

"She has." Goddard rubbed at his chin again. "Have we heard back from Spero yet?"

"No, sir. Shall I—"

There was a knock at the door, and Jordan immediately sprang from his chair, PDA still perched on his palm. He strolled across the room, twisted the handle and allowed a few inches of space to see who was bothering them and why. Apparently satisfied with the reason, Jordan stepped back and allowed the man to enter.

It was Spero. He strolled past Jordan and held up a plain manila folder.

"Just in time. We were about to call out the search and rescue team to find you." Goddard reached for the file. He admired the scar that started on the right side of Spero's forehead and traveled well past his jaw. "What did you find?"

"Very little, sir." Spero remained standing with his hands clasped in front of him. He spoke as though he were reading off a dossier floating in mid-air between them. "Jack Smith. Former Marine. Disappeared for a few years. Resurfaced recently. Appears to be an independent contractor. He's taken out some high-profile targets. No official channels are aware of his record, but I talked to some of my own contacts and unofficially he checks out. For our purposes, he's clean."

"Smith?" Goddard raised an eyebrow.

"Alias." Spero tilted his head and shrugged. "It's common, especially for his line of work. Sometimes they only go by their monikers, but Jack doesn't seem to have one."

Goddard flipped through the contents of the folder. "The file is relatively thin, no?"

Spero shifted his weight from one foot to another. "There wasn't a lot of dirt to dig up. Jack appears to be quite good at his job. He goes in, he does what needs to be done, he gets out. No complications. No need for a clean-up crew because he had to kill a maid or a neighbor or a pet parakeet. He doesn't take many jobs, but the contracts he has are all worth millions. He seems to be the one you call in when no one else can or wants to do the job. This guy doesn't care about risks, and therefore they don't affect him."

Goddard nodded and scanned the papers inside the folder one more time. He pinned them down with his thumb so that the warm ocean breeze blowing through the suite wouldn't send them flying. He knew some of Jack's previous targets, had even benefited from a few of their deaths. The fact that he had no idea who had taken out those men was a testament to Jack's abilities as an assassin. He could prove to be quite useful to them.

"And how do you feel about the idea of bringing Jack on board, Spero?"

Spero shifted his gaze from his boss to the window, where outside the sun was shining against a bright blue, cloudless sky. After a moment he returned his attention to the senator. "It's a risk. We don't know much about him."

"But you can keep digging?"

"I can, but given the results from my initial investigation, I expect the results to be fruitless."

"Have you found any connection between Jack and our Michelle?"

"No, sir." Spero looked confused. "He tends to keep to himself, working alone. He's been known to have an associate or two, but it seems to be out of convenience rather than loyalty."

"Michelle says they go way back."

"I have not found any evidence of that, sir."

"Very well." Goddard tossed the file onto his desk. "I'll meet you out front in an hour."

"Sir," Spero said, with a nod of his head. He turned and let himself out of Goddard's office.

"It's peculiar Michelle did not show up anywhere," Jordan said.

"Possibly." Goddard was not one to trust easily, but Michelle had singlehandedly carried his books for several years. She had everything on him. But here he stood, a free man. If he couldn't trust her, then he'd be left with very few friends. "But in this business names change and so does one's direction in life."

"Still, we must be careful, sir."

Goddard took a moment to himself before standing up and turning to the window. The reflection showed that Jordan had also stood, ready for his next instruction. "Put Vasquez on the case. I trust Spero, but this is what Vasquez does for a living. If there is something to find, he'll find it."

"Yes, sir."

Goddard could already hear Jordan tapping furiously at his device. "And call Michelle back. Have her invite Jack to our next meeting."

"It'll be a risk, sir. If he is not who he says he is, he could cause trouble."

"He already knows who I am," Goddard said. "And Michelle has proven at least the benefit of the doubt, hasn't she?"

"Of course, sir." Jordan still sounded reluctant.

Goddard turned from the window and crossed the room, clasping Jordan on the shoulder. "I know you're just looking out for me, and I appreciate it. But I didn't get to where I am today without taking a few risks."

Jordan nodded and finished off his message to Michelle. "Anything else, sir?"

"A change of clothes. The white suit." Goddard wanted a very specific message to be conveyed with this trip to visit Martinez. "And tell Spero it'll be his job to keep an eye on Jack while we're there. We must find a way to test his loyalty without turning him away."

Jordan nodded and left the room, set to do exactly as he was told. If only everyone could be as efficient and reliable, perhaps they wouldn't be in this situation with Martinez to begin with.

CHAPTER TWELVE

"How is Costa Rica treating you so far, Jack?" Goddard was riding shotgun in the vehicle, while Jack and Sadie sat in the back. The seats were made from some of the softest leather Jack had ever felt. All four windows were cracked a couple of inches. The smell of grilled sausage from a nearby street cart filled the cabin.

Jack was wired, though the connection did not go both ways. They wanted Bear to hear everything that went down today, but they needed a minimal amount of tech on them in case Goddard got spooked and decided to do a sweep. The tiny mic placed under the collar of Jack's shirt would be undetectable.

"Pretty damn good, sir." Jack cast a glance in Sadie's direction. He noted that Goddard caught sight of it. The two were playing up the 'old friends' angle, and the more it seemed like something was going on between them, the more likely Goddard would be willing to trust him.

Except Jack still didn't trust her. She was CIA. Jack and the Agency hadn't seen eye to eye since he'd left the CIA-sponsored program he had been indoctrinated into at the age of eighteen. For all he knew, once their op was over, Sadie would haul him and Bear in and see what charges they could get to stick. It wouldn't be many, but after everything he'd done over the course of his career, even one could provide him with a life sentence.

Then again Sadie was putting her life on the line, too. She had spent years under Martinez's wing, finally working her way up to getting into Goddard's good graces. She begrudgingly accepted Jack's and Bear's help. The idea that her boss wanted everyone in on this meant Goddard wouldn't be easy to take down, especially now with the complication of Javier's daughter having been taken.

The morning hadn't treated Javier any better. He hadn't appeared to have slept the night before. His clothes were wrinkled and smelled of day old sweat. His bloodshot eyes drooped, standing out against the dark circles under his eyes. With every minute his daughter was still missing, Javier grew more desperate. A desperate man was a dangerous man, and Jack and Sadie certainly didn't need that kind of complication now that they were entering the lion's den.

And Bear wanted things to get more interesting...

The SUV pulled to a stop and Jack glanced over their destination. He had been informed during the ride that they were heading to Mateo Martinez's personal residence. As far as houses belonging to drug lords went, this one was understated. It was well-concealed behind an array of meticulously groomed shrubs and bushes. Sprawling colorful gardens circled a stone stairway that led up to the front of the house. The façade was ornate, made of wood and stone, but much smaller than Jack had anticipated. From what he had learned of the cartel leader, Martinez was an excellent businessman, and conservative by nature. He didn't invest more than necessary in his home. Rather he put it back into his empire to build it up further.

Goddard, Jack, and Sadie exited the vehicle while the senator's driver stayed behind. It was mid-afternoon now and the sun glared down without obstruction. Goddard was wearing a white suit and hat, but seemed to be acclimated to the humid weather. Jack could already feel himself sweating through his thin cotton shirt. Sadie looked comfortable in her short red dress. She had shifted into her light and carefree mode as soon as Goddard's man had picked them up, and she hadn't let up since. He was used to working with chameleons, but she was one of the best.

A second sedan pulled up a few moments later. Three of Goddard's men joined them, as well as the personal assistant Jack had seen the other night at the restaurant. The first man was introduced as Spero, head of the senator's personal security contingent. The other two were Reynard, who had closely cropped red hair and high cheekbones, and McGinnis, who had jet black hair and a thick mustache. The men said little.

Spero looked down at his phone, and then up again at the front entrance to the house. "Wait here a moment, sir."

Goddard nodded his head and turned toward the rose bushes lining the driveway. "What do you think of the gardens, Michelle?"

Sadie's light accent returned when she addressed Goddard. "Every time I see them, I find them even more beautiful."

Goddard swept his arm toward the house. "Jack, you came at a perfect time to see the wonder of this place."

"Flowers aren't exactly my thing." He kept his gaze fixed on the home, watching the entrances and the roof. *Why weren't there more men out here?*

"We shouldn't overlook nature's beauty just because we often find ourselves busy with work. It's important to find balance."

"Never would have pegged you as the philosophical type." Jack shrugged his shoulders. "Anyway, I like finding nature's beauty at the bottom of a glass. Though that doesn't usually lend itself to having balance."

Goddard laughed at the same time as one of his men's phones rang out. McGinnis lifted it to his ear, shot a look toward Reynard, and the two of them hurried off after Spero. Goddard's gaze followed them inside the building, but he didn't look particularly concerned.

The senator was an interesting creature. He had all the power in a situation like this, but he put full trust in his men. The assistant appeared to have all of Goddard's plans at the tip of his fingers, legal and otherwise. Spero and his men were tasked with keeping the senator safe, which couldn't be an easy job considering everything Goddard had his hands in. How much did they know?

The man himself wasn't particularly imposing. He was older, lean without being muscular, and more than likely wasn't carrying. His furrowed brow and tight lips made him look serious, but he had the ability to become jovial at the drop of a hat. He turned his back on Jack as if he had no worry in the world that this stranger could end his life right then and there.

And he could. It'd be one of the simplest jobs yet. He could reach out and snap Goddard's neck and take out the assistant in a couple of blows. Wouldn't even need Sadie's help. The other men had left. By the time they returned only the bodies would remain. The only other protection Goddard had was from the driver. By the time the man exited his vehicle and drew on them, either Jack or Sadie would've already taken out the others and made their move toward the car. They could be out of there in less than two minutes. Mission accomplished.

Sadie caught Jack's eye and shook her head slightly, as if she knew exactly what was running through his mind. A spike of annoyance coursed through his body, but as quickly as it arrived, it was gone. Their first mission was to find Javier's daughter. Taking out Goddard would not ensure they'd be able to do that. It'd reduce their chances to zero.

Before the senator found something else of no consequence to comment on, Spero jogged down the sidewalk, gun drawn. Jack couldn't help the flinch that rocked his body as he went for his own weapon, only to remember that he and Sadie were unarmed. It was an act of faith that could get them both killed.

Goddard picked up on his apprehension. He held up his hand with a tight smile on his face. "You're safe here, Jack," he said, before turning to his man. "What happened?"

"They're all dead." Spero sucked in short, quick bursts of air, catching his breath. He was on high alert but not panicked. He had been trained well.

"Is the house clear?"

"Yes, sir."

"Show me."

Spero led them up the front stairs. The smell of death greeted them before they were through the main entrance. The air felt heavy and still.

The group remained quiet as they were guided through the foyer and into the main sitting room where the stark white furniture had been painted with crimson. Six bodies lay haphazardly across the floor. All had bullet wounds to the head or chest. In some cases, both.

Sadie let out a gasp and held her hands to her mouth. She took a step closer to Jack and leaned against him. He automatically wrapped an arm around her shoulder. But when he looked down at her he saw no fear in her eyes. It was an act. Sadie had seen plenty of dead bodies in her lifetime, but it didn't mean Michelle had.

Jack saw a side to Goddard he hadn't yet, and it made him rethink the kind of person the senator was. He showed no shock or discomfort over being at the site of a massacre. Instead, he turned clinical as he inspected each body.

"Do we know what happened here?"

Spero and his men exchanged a glance, but when Goddard's head of security opened his mouth, nothing came out. Goddard looked up at him, and his expression revealed his disappointment.

"Is Martinez here?" Jack let go of Sadie and stepped forward.

Goddard eyed Jack for a moment before nodding and pointing down to the body he was standing over. It was the only body with non-fatal wounds. Both of his knee caps had been shot out before he got a bullet to the brain. They wanted him to watch as the others were executed.

"My guess is Martinez knew the shooter."

"Why?" Goddard stood up and turned his full attention onto Jack.

Jack ignored the stares of the room and paced along its perimeter, taking in all the information he could. "Martinez was disabled before he was killed. There are five other men in this room, but three of them were clearly stationed outside, given their clothes and their larger weapons. They were probably the guards that should have met us out front as we pulled in."

Goddard looked over at Spero, who nodded and pointed at a man across the room. "Gutierrez should've been there to lead us inside."

Jack continued his circuit around the room. "My guess is the shooter was invited inside to meet with Martinez and two of his closest advisors. He took Martinez out first, but didn't kill him. Then he took out the two advisors with a pair of bullets to the chest each. When the shots were heard, Gutierrez and two of his closest men came rushing in. The shooter was ready for them and took them out before they could get off any shots of their own."

"Why keep Martinez alive?" Goddard asked.

"The shooter's business was with him. He wanted to send a message before he killed him, maybe let him think he might survive the ordeal if he talked. The gunman only disabled him so he'd have time to go back and speak with him after everyone was dead. Once the message was relayed, Martinez joined the dead."

Reynard spoke up for the first time since Jack had met him. "There are three more men upstairs. Two on the roof. All dead."

Jack looked back over his shoulder, as if he could see through the walls and up to the second floor. "Any dead on the staircase?"

Reynard shook his head.

"The shooter had a team then. They knew the layout of the building and where all the men would be stationed. He probably came in with three or four guys, who headed upstairs while their boss conducted his business. The lackeys took out the guys upstairs and on the roof so no one could come to Martinez's rescue when the shooter open fired."

"Impressive," Goddard said.

Jack shrugged. "I've been around a lot of murder scenes. Besides, knowing how the other guys think has kept me alive all these years."

"Congratulations," Goddard said, and it sounded like he meant it. He then turned to his assistant. "Jordan, make the appropriate arrangements to deal with this mess."

"Already on it, sir."

Goddard stepped over a body and placed a gentle hand on Sadie's shoulder. She had built herself up to have tears in her eyes now. "I'm sorry you had to see that, Michelle. I usually try to keep you out of such situations."

"It's all right." There was a waiver to her voice. Jack couldn't help but be impressed. "Should I collect the books?"

"Yes." Goddard looked down at the phone buzzing in his hand. Jack managed to catch the name Vasquez before Goddard answered it. "Excuse me." He exited the house through the front door.

Jack peered around the room to figure out if this worked out in their favor or not. He turned to Jordan. He was clearly in charge while the senator was out of the room despite only being Goddard's assistant. Even Spero himself deferred to the young assistant.

"What next?" Jack asked.

Jordan looked around the room and then met Jack's gaze. His finger hovered over the screen of his ever-present PDA. "Do you have room in your schedule for one more contract?"

CHAPTER THIRTEEN

After retrieving Martinez's books from the locked cabinet in his office, Sadie allowed herself to be guided out through the main doors by Reynard, who kept a gentle hand on her shoulder. She fought against her instinct to break his arm. She let her eyes glaze over while keeping Jack in view at all times. It was easy to trick the others into believing she was just a woman who was good at math who wasn't used to seeing the carnage of the business she was so entrenched in.

But Jack saw right through her. She wasn't sure if she liked that feeling or if it bothered her that she couldn't trick him as well. He got on her nerves more often than not, but she couldn't deny she was as impressed as Goddard had been when he'd read the room earlier. They knew odds-on favorite for the shooter was Martinez's nephew, Nicolás—he fit the description of being familiar to the leader of the cartel—but Jack had done a good job of making it seem like he was in the dark about that detail.

She shouldn't be working with Jack. She liked living life by the rules, even if they weren't the societal norm. It had helped her get to this point. Jack was as wild a card as they came. Riley was a bit easier to deal with, but both of them had a reputation of using the rulebook as a coaster.

They were both professionals, though. And it would be in her favor to remember that. Jack knew what he was doing, and as long as he didn't step over a line and put her own op in jeopardy, she'd have to trust that he was the key to bringing down Goddard for good. They just had to bide their time until someone discovered the whereabouts of Javier's daughter.

They stepped into a cloud of dust that clung to Sadie's damp skin and proceeded past the gardens and bushes and shrubs. They looked less vibrant now. The life had been sucked out of not only the dead men inside, but also the lush surroundings.

Goddard hung up the phone as soon as they approached him outside the car. His eyes flitted to Jordan, who glanced at Jack before returning his attention to his boss and nodding. The senator tucked his phone back into his pocket and then stretched his hand toward Jack. Jack grasped it with an eyebrow raised.

"I'm sure it'll come as no surprise to you that we had you vetted, despite Michelle's high recommendation."

"Trust but verify," Jack said.

Goddard patted him on the back before opening the door for Sadie. "Exactly. You'll be happy to hear that your record is highly regarded. We could use someone like you on our team."

"I don't tend to stay in place for too long."

"And how long do you plan to stay here in Costa Rica?"

Jack caught Sadie's eye, but she let nothing slip. Under the watchful eye of Jordan, Spero, and the others, she couldn't risk giving him any kind of signal.

Jack turned back to Goddard. "I don't plan on leaving just yet."

"Good to hear, good to hear." Goddard sounded delighted, but there was a pull at his lips that Michelle knew meant something was not sitting well with him. Was it Jack's behavior? Was it hers? Or was it the fact that Mateo Martinez's brains were currently splattered across a vintage tea set in the man's own living room?

"Sir," Jordan interrupted, tapping his watch.

"Right, right." Goddard seemed flustered for the first time today, but he straightened his jacket and gathered himself again. "It's time to pay a visit to one of my associates. I would like you to join us, Jack."

Jack followed Sadie into the back of the car as Goddard got in the front. "Would this associate happen to be the one responsible for the scene we just witnessed?"

"There's a high probability." Goddard turned to the driver. "Swing by Michelle's place first, Marcus. I'd rather she not join us today."

Sadie immediately sat up in her chair. "Thomas."

Goddard twisted around in his seat. He'd always had a fatherly affection for her, which had made it much easier to gain his trust. A seductress was rarely trustworthy the moment she couldn't get what she wanted, but a daughter was forever loyal. "It's for your own safety, Michelle."

Jack placed a hand on Sadie's arm. Goddard glanced down at the gesture.

"He's right," Jack said. "If this guy is the one who took out Martinez, he could be looking for an all-out war."

Sadie couldn't help the piercing look she gave him as she shrugged off his arm. She turned back to Goddard. It was time to take a risk. "It's Nicolás, isn't it?"

"And why would you think that?" Goddard's face tightened.

"There are always rumors. I know Nicolás. He's a hothead. He loves his uncle, but he loves power more. I wouldn't be surprised if he was the one who did this."

Goddard sighed. "Nicolás is likely the culprit. I've been advised to take him out of the picture due to the instability that would reign with him as a leader." Goddard took a moment. "Since you know him so well, what would you suggest?"

Sadie's body tensed. She knew Goddard would listen to her, but she had to weigh her options here. On the one hand, she could suggest they take Nicolás out of the picture. It was what Goddard wanted to do, and it'd be one less drug lord in the world. It would also further chip away at the foundation of the senator's little empire, which would make it easier to take down the whole operation.

On the other hand, Nicolás could prove useful to her. He was a hot head, yes, but he was young and naive. He'd been in the business for a while, thanks to his uncle and his father, but he still had a lot to learn. He could be manipulated, and while Goddard may see Sadie as a daughter, Nicolás had always had a much more lustful interest in her. She could play that to their advantage.

All of this went through Sadie's head in a couple of seconds. Her hesitation to answer Goddard was natural. She twisted her lips, as if she were truly struggling with admitting what she was about to say.

"Nicolás has always been kind to me, but what he did to his uncle is unacceptable. I know you have a reputation to maintain." She paused briefly. "Then again, he may prove useful."

"How so?"

"A figurehead?" Jack said.

Sadie felt a spike of annoyance at him. If he didn't keep his mouth shut, he could ruin her whole tactic. "Figureheads don't last long in this business, but they can prove useful. If you keep Nicolás alive long enough to find someone who is a better fit, you may be able to save yourself from plenty of headaches."

It was a risk for Sadie and her team back at Langley. Helping to stabilize Goddard's operation could hurt them in the future, but not doing so could get a lot more people killed. They were after Goddard and anyone else who deserved to be held responsible for their actions. She wasn't looking to start an all-out war.

"You'll be the one to speak to him?" Goddard asked.

Jack leaned forward, unable to hide his concern. "Sir."

Goddard merely raised a hand and held Sadie's gaze.

She swallowed audibly before answering. This could easily blow up in their faces, but what choice did she have at this point? "Yes," she answered. "I'll talk to him."

CHAPTER FOURTEEN

I hung back as I saw Jack and Sadie enter the small compound on the outskirts of San José. A small tracking device planted on the inside of Jack's shoe had allowed me to follow them without being spotted. I could travel several streets over without worrying about losing them. It was a risk being this close to the buildings, but I'd cleared the woods surrounding them. I had to take my chances. If something went wrong, I had to be close.

I knew who was on the other side of those doors. Sadie had briefed us this morning about Nicolás Garcia, Martinez's nephew, just in case he came into play. Turns out he came into play in a big way after Martinez's body was discovered. I had heard the entire conversation about the crime scene, as well as the back and forth between Goddard, Sadie, and Jack. I knew Jack was trying to keep Sadie out of a sticky situation, but I also knew Sadie wouldn't take any of his shit. She was tough, and she had already proven she could stay in character whenever a curveball was thrown her way.

Besides, she had a legitimate excuse to be the one to speak with Nicolás. If Goddard barged in there with them, the situation was likely to blow up. At least this way Sadie and Jack could control the narrative and attempt to guide it in a favorable direction. Martinez was out of the picture now, and that was an unstable enough environment for Javier's kid, but if someone decided to start a beef with Nicolás, it was unlikely the girl would survive for much longer. As long as Camila was in play, all of their movements were restricted.

I heard muffled words in the background before Sadie's clear voice sounded in my ear. "Nicolás."

I kept alert to my surroundings as the scene unfolded in my mind's eye. I heard the sound of kissing and saw in my imagination that Sadie had leaned forward to peck Nicolás on his cheeks.

Nicolás spoke in Spanish. "Michelle. Who is your friend?"

Sadie responded in kind. "Jack. You can trust him. He's an old friend. He's here to keep me safe."

There was a momentary pause before Nicolás spoke again. I imagined him looking Jack up and down, assessing him. "You don't trust me to keep you safe?"

"It's not you I'm worried about. It's Goddard."

The pair were still speaking in Spanish, but Jack's ears would perk up at Goddard's name. I willed him to keep calm despite not knowing what the two were saying. Sadie would likely switch over to English soon enough.

"Why are you worried about him?"

There was a pause. "May I speak in English?" Nicolás must have nodded after a moment's hesitation, as she continued on in a language Jack could actually understand. Her light accent was still in place. "Goddard sent me here to talk to you."

It was a bold move. Sadie was playing triple agent right now, and she'd have to walk a fine line to make sure none of the other parties became privy to her game.

"About my uncle?" Nicolás's accent was much heavier.

"Yes. He believes you had something to do with it."

There was a clinking of ice in a glass. Nicolás's voice sounded further away now. "And what do you believe?"

"I know you killed him, Nicolás. I thought we talked about this. I thought we decided—"

Sadie broke off with a small intake of breath. There was a beat and then Nicolás said, "Leave us."

Two pairs of footsteps exited the room, followed by the click of a door.

"I thought we decided to wait. That it would be best to find another way to work your way up."

"A man must take what he deserves."

"This will have consequences."

"I am aware of the consequences." Nicolás voice moved closer. "Do you doubt me?"

"Hey, man," Jack said.

There was a rustling, as if Sadie had put her hand out to stop him from moving forward and had brushed the mic under his collar. "Jack, it's fine."

"Who is this man?" Nicolás asked again.

"Just a friend." Sadie's voice took on a softer tone. "I'm just worried. What's going to happen next? Will it be safe for us?"

"No one will touch us once we take over my uncle's empire. You'll have everything you've ever wanted. You won't have to work for him anymore."

"And Goddard?"

"That old man is useful, for now. He has to stay in the picture until I can find a way to remove him myself. The old bastard doesn't know how lucky he is."

I heard a branch snap behind me and whirled around, ducking down as far as my huge frame would allow me. My eyes scanned the trees until they fell upon a figure walking parallel to my position. He was dressed in black with an AK-47 slung over his shoulder. He yawned widely and kicked a rock out of his way. Some patrolman.

If I stayed still, it was likely he'd pass right by me and I wouldn't have to deal with a confrontation. I was armed, but if either one of us fired our weapons, Nicolás's men would know someone was out here.

That would put Jack and Sadie in danger. Not to mention I wasn't sure I'd be able to high tail it out of there before I had someone else on my ass.

I was half-tuned into what Sadie was saying to Nicolás. She was asking him what she should say to Goddard. How could she convince the senator not to take Nicolás out right now? How could he prove useful?

Nicolás laughed. "Let him come at me. I'm not afraid of the American."

"You don't need a war right now, Nicolás. Everything is unstable as it is. Play by Goddard's rules for now and you'll benefit in the long run. I have Mateo's books. If we bide our time, we can cut Goddard out completely."

If Nicolás was smart, he'd follow Sadie's suggestions. She was giving him a way to keep what he had taken without having to fend off the big boss. Goddard wouldn't like keeping Nicolás in the equation for long, but once they found a better suited leader for the cartel, then Martinez's nephew could be dealt with.

The patrolman had just passed my hiding spot behind a large tree, its roots spreading out like fingers all around me, when my phone began to buzz in my pocket. The woods weren't quiet by any means, but it sounded like an alarm was going off. The man stopped and tilted his head to the side. He heard it.

I shoved my hand in my pocket and clicked one of the buttons along the side, not even bothering to check who was calling me. Not just anyone had the number, so the call was important. But at the moment I had more pressing matters to deal with.

The bored patrolman remained alert. As soon as he started turning in my direction, I dipped behind the tree and waited. His footsteps crunched on sticks and dead leaves. He was an amateur and would pay for it with his life. But as young as he was, I felt no guilt. If it was him or me, I wasn't going to go down without a fight.

Sadie's voice still sounded in my ear, but I pushed it to the back of my mind as I concentrated on the barrel of his rifle appearing around the tree. I dropped to a knee and struck at the man's groin as soon as he was within reach. There was a grunt and then he dropped to the ground. His grip loosened on his weapon. I yanked it out of his hand and tossed it a few feet away.

He may have been an amateur, but the kid could fight, and he was quick. He was out of breath from the blow, but he was already recovering. He blocked my next shot and crawled away and tried reaching for his gun. I rushed ahead and kicked it out of the way and brought my knee up to his chest. He landed on his back but was already scrambling away as I took two steps toward him.

He kicked up at me. I dodged his foot and drove mine down on his knee. I leaned down to wrap my hands around his neck. His hand shot out, a glint of silver winking at me as he went for my jugular. I whipped my head out of the way and gripped his arm in my hand, pinning him down with my knee on his chest. He was fast, but I was nearly twice his size, and there was no way he was getting out from under me. I pulled the knife from his hand and plunged it into his neck, quickly and effortlessly. He was gone before I pulled it clear.

The buzzing in my pocket resumed. I wiped my hands on the kid's vest and pulled out my cell, not even bothering to look at who was calling. It could only be one of three people at this number, and they each knew a phone call risked my life.

"This better be good. You nearly got me killed."

It was Javier. His voice was strained. "They found a body."

CHAPTER FIFTEEN

I rolled the window of the Land Rover all the way down and stuck my elbow outside, feeling the hot sun and mild breeze along my arm. I spotted Jack and Sadie making their way toward me, silent and looking harried. Goddard had them dropped off at Sadie's place, and I'd followed behind at a distance. Once the coast was clear, I'd called Jack and told him what Javier had said.

Jack slid into the front, while Sadie scooted across the seat in the back to sit in the middle so she could lean forward and listen better.

"News?" Jack asked.

I shook my head. "Javier's been up my ass. They're not going in without us. Time to move out."

"Got away as soon as we could, big man."

"I know. He's just worried about his kid."

"Can't blame him."

The trip was made in relative silence, punctuated by a discussion here or there over what would happen between Goddard and Nicolás should one of them decide to do the unexpected. We all agreed it would be disastrous. If they played their parts, we might be able to save this op.

But as the conversation died out, I could tell all of our minds focused on what lay ahead. Javier had called to tell me the same men who had taken Camila had sent another video, this time of the body of a young girl. Her face was never shown, and they couldn't tell whether she had been killed or just badly beaten, but she matched Camila's description.

Except the men had slipped up in the video. It was a different warehouse than the last one, and the crates had identification numbers printed on every side. They were specific to a certain company, and from there, it was just a matter of narrowing it down. Javier had called in his men to secure the perimeter to make sure no one went in or out. He was waiting for us to show up before he moved in.

Javier was a tough man, but when it comes to your children's lives, no one is that strong. I could tell he didn't want to admit it, but he was putting off the inevitable. He was doing whatever he could to delay going into that warehouse and finding out whether his daughter was still alive.

I pulled up alongside the road and threw the Rover in park. The three of us took in our surroundings, looking for anything out of the ordinary. If Jack or Sadie were caught working with Javier, the whole op would be a wrap. But Javier's men had arrived ahead of time to sweep the area and disable any security cameras. The scene was clean.

I pulled the latch and pushed out against the door. It smelled like where they dumped the waste from dragging the seabed. The breeze swept across my skin and cooled me down after a long and stifling ride in the car. I could tell Jack and Sadie were doing the same. The moment was brief as Javier stepped around one of the cars, a pained look on his face.

"Are you ready?"

The three of us pulled our weapons. I'd had my Springfield XD .45 on me all day, but Jack was sporting a backup Glock 9mm from Sadie's apartment. It wasn't ideal, but we had all agreed it was smarter to get to the warehouse as soon as possible. Javier's mental stability couldn't take much more.

We followed Javier around several cars and to the front of a small metal building. Everyone had been instructed to stay out of sight. If the girl was still alive we didn't want to risk further injury. If she was dead we wanted to get the jump on the bastards who did this to a ten-year-old child.

The building's sides were dull and rusting, but the sun glinted off the metal roof and struck me in the eyes. I squinted against the glare and tried to gauge the warehouse's layout.

"It's one large room, with a smaller office off to the right." Javier pointed to a corner of the building. "I don't know what's on the other side of that door."

He was talking about the possibility of the kidnappers still being present, but I knew he was thinking of his daughter. I clasped him on the shoulder before taking point. "We'll get it done."

As the four of us moved in, firearms drawn, Javier's men closed around the building. We didn't have to worry about open fire coming from the roof or the surrounding area, but as soon as we were through that door, we were walking into the unknown.

When we reached the building the four of us flattened ourselves against the façade. I leaned my head against the cool metal and waited, breath held. There was no noise coming from within but that didn't mean the building was empty. It might just mean whoever was inside was ready for us. I figured it wouldn't be a person on the other side. The right explosives would do the job well enough.

I shuffled forward until I was within arm's reach of the door. I heard the others follow my lead. When everyone had stopped, I turned back to them. "Jack and I will take the middle, Sadie goes right, Jav goes left." I turned my gaze on Javier directly. "If you spot the girl, don't stop to check her until we know the building is clear. We won't be doing her any favors if we miss someone."

Javier nodded first, followed by the other two. I turned back to the door, and on a silent count of three wrenched it open, .45 up, body tensed. Dusty air billowed out. The four of us fanned out to scout the area.

It was dead silent inside. There was no airflow on the ground. Crates were stacked in neat rows throughout the warehouse, with twisting aisles providing plenty of cover for whoever might be hiding from us.

I nodded to the others. "Clear the room and meet at the back wall."

We each crept forward ready for whatever might come at us. My hands were steady despite my elevated heartbeat. The adrenaline zeroed my focus as I made my way between the stacks of crates.

The boxes were long and thin, but dozens of them stacked together meant the piles were well over my head. I kept an eye out for any movement from above. It was unlikely anyone could bounce from stack to stack without being noticed. That didn't mean they wouldn't try. Having an aerial view of your enemies would be worth the risk.

As silent as everyone was, I heard the others making their way through the room. We were like mice making our way through a maze. There'd be a pause in footsteps and a quick rustle of clothes as someone turned a corner to look down the next aisle. The room was so silent, I could even hear Jack's breathing when our paths neared each other.

Methodically, we swept the room. When I reached the back wall I waited until the others came into view before calling the all-clear on my end. They each parroted the sentiment. The warehouse was empty.

"Did anyone find the girl?" I asked.

Javier looked pale as he stood in a thin beam of sunlight coming in from a small window near the roof.

Jack gestured down the aisle he had emerged from. He said bluntly, "Down here."

The four of us followed his lead with our guns out despite the reassurance that we were alone. The center of the room had been cleared out, the boxes pushed back to make a wider opening. In the center, directly under one of the lights that hung from the ceiling, as if she were under a spotlight, was a young girl in a white dress. It had tiny flowers on it some of which matched the color of her light brown hair. Her back was to us, her knees drawn up to her chest. Her skin was ashen.

Javier stepped forward, peering down at the girl for a moment, his breath ragged. The three of us stood still, waiting for his lead. After a moment Sadie holstered her gun and walked up to him. She placed a hand on his forearm.

"You don't have to be here." Her soft voice echoed around the room.

Javier took a step forward. He reached his hand out and faltered. His knees began to buckle. "I can't. I can't."

"You don't have to," Sadie said.

Javier looked up, his gaze meeting Jack's. No words were needed. Jack nodded his head once, and then turned the body. He squatted down and pulled at her shoulder to gently lay her on her back. The body gave no resistance. If we hadn't already known she was dead this would have been a confirmation. Jack swept hair out of her face.

Javier let out a strangled groan and fell to his knees. Sadie followed him, holding his shoulders. I took a step forward, unsure what I should do or say. He was rocking back and forth.

"It's not her," he said. "It's not her. It's not her."

CHAPTER SIXTEEN

J avier sat back on his haunches and after a few minutes he was able to speak again. I watched the change in his demeanor as hope reentered his body. His daughter was still alive, and it provided the energy he needed to regain his composure.

"Her name was Marianna." His voice was low and gravely. "She was friends with my daughter. I didn't even know she was missing."

"Do you think they were taken at the same time?"

Javier got to his feet. "No. They would've included her in on the video."

"Then why take her now?" Sadie asked.

"It's a warning." Javier paced back and forth. "Camila is still alive, but we can't count on it being for long. Not after this."

Anger welled as I stared at the young girl. I shifted my gaze to Javier. "We'll find her."

When Javier looked up at me, his eyes were wild. "We don't have much time. Whoever has taken her wants us to back off. They know we're working with Goddard still. They must assume we're just biding our time."

Jack gripped the back of his neck. "We're gonna have to be careful. You need to fall back."

Javier strode over to Jack and went toe-to-toe with him. "This is my daughter."

Jack held up his hands. "I know, man. I know. I can't even imagine what you're going through right now, but the fact of the matter is we need to play this right. One wrong move and something terrible could happen. You need to trust us to get the job done."

Javier deflated. "I understand." He let out a deep sigh. "I just don't understand who could know."

"What are the chances of a leak in your department?" I asked.

Javier looked like he was going to immediately dismiss the idea, but thought better of it. This was his daughter. There was no room for pride. "It's possible," he said. "But unlikely. My team is close. They've been working together for years. We have a good system, a good rapport."

"It wouldn't hurt to take a closer look, just to make sure."

Javier just bobbed his head up and down. He had resumed pacing.

Sadie turned to Jack. "Do you have any idea who could've taken her?"

Jack rubbed the back of his neck again. "Who would benefit from keeping Goddard alive?"

I laughed. "Goddard?"

"If he knew who I was, would he bring me in even closer? Why not take me out when he had the chance? He practically ran that restaurant. Or even in the car earlier today?"

"Could be wondering who you work for."

"He took Javier's daughter. Whoever it is already assumes I'm working for him."

"Or with him," Sadie offered. "There's a difference. He might want to know who you report to."

I watched as Javier walked a couple steps away and pulled out his phone, presumably to call his men in to take away the body. My gaze returned to Sadie. "Have you heard anything?"

She shook her head. "Nothing. I know Goddard called Vasquez to confirm your identity, but he hadn't told me anything he found. I assume it all checked out with them."

"Unless Vasquez has some serious contacts, he wouldn't find anything on me but the basics. Good dossier for an assassin. Goddard would be intrigued by that. Sounds like he already is."

"Goddard isn't accustomed to taking risks that wouldn't guarantee at least some sort of profit." I looked up as Javier's men walked down the stacks. They carried a body bag with them.

"It'd be safer for him to take me out. So who wants Goddard alive and still wants me in the picture?"

Sadie stepped out of the way as the men picked up the body and placed her within the bag, zipping it shut with a resounding finality. "Someone who isn't sure how much longer Goddard can be useful to them."

"Let's move out," Javier said. "We can't stay here for much longer without drawing unwanted attention."

The four of us followed Javier's men out of the warehouse and watched as they placed Marianna in the back of one of the cars. She deserved better than this, but it was as good as it was going to get.

I turned to Javier. "Do you know her family?"

He rubbed a hand over his tired face. "She lived with her mother and grandmother. Her father died when she was an infant. They were good people, always kind to Camila. She always had a home with them."

"They'll have to be informed," Sadie said.

Javier sounded like he was slipping inside himself. He pulled his phone out of his pocket. "I'll do it."

Sadie placed a gentle hand over the top of his. "In person. They'll appreciate it."

Javier nodded absentmindedly and moved toward his car. I didn't envy the task he had ahead of him. I couldn't imagine the thoughts that would pervade his mind the remainder of the day.

Jack followed the man's movements. "Someone should go with him."

Sadie followed him. "I'll talk to one of his men and meet you at the car in a minute."

Jack and I broke off from the crowd and headed back to the Land Rover. The murmur of voices behind us faded as Javier's team dispersed. I kept an eye on the surrounding woods in case someone appeared. I couldn't put it past these bastards to keep someone nearby to gather intelligence on all of the players involved.

"What do you think, big man?"

I ran a hand across the top of my head. "How did everything get so screwed up? It was supposed to be an easy op. Point and shoot."

"That should've been our first warning. They're never that easy."

"Ain't that the truth."

"If we were still in that pizza parlor in Miami, I'd slap ourselves upside the head."

Jack pulled a pair of sunglasses out of his breast pocket and pushed them onto his face. "I'd still steal these from Thorne."

I chuckled, but the humor didn't last long. "Think Frank could be wrapped up in all this?"

Jack took a moment before he answered. "I honestly don't know, man. It wouldn't make much sense to send us on a mission and then pull it out from underneath us without giving a heads up."

"Things change. The CIA is involved now."

Jack checked over his shoulder. Sadie was still chatting with Javier's men. "You know I don't trust Frank, but I don't think he'd waste our time like this. He wants Goddard dead. If he didn't, the CIA would be all over this and the good senator would end up in a cell instead of a grave."

"Back to square one, then." We'd arrived at the Rover. I leaned against the driver's side door and watched as Sadie shook one of the soldier's hands and then jogged back over to us.

"Javier is heading over to Marianna's house now," she said. "A couple of his guys are going with him."

I followed his car as they pulled away and roared off down the road. "He didn't look too good in there."

"It's a rollercoaster," Sadie said. "Worry that Marianna was actually Camila, and then relieved when she wasn't. Devastated his daughter lost a friend and another girl had to pay the price for the life he leads. Then back to worrying over whether Camila is alive."

Jack walked around to the passenger side door. "She doesn't have much time left. We can't afford for you to back off Goddard and risk him thinking something's up. We have to find the girl before we can take care of him."

Sadie didn't offer any hope. She opened the rear driver's side door and climbed in. Jack and I followed. I turned the key and listened for the now-familiar roar of the engine. The vehicle was reliable, if not completely inconspicuous. For now it was all we had.

"Son of a bitch." Jack slapped the dash, bringing me out of my reverie.

"What's wrong?" I glanced at Sadie in the rearview, but she looked just as surprised as I felt. Both of us were on high alert. I reached for my Springfield.

Jack backhanded my shoulder and I relaxed. There was a manic grin spread across his face.

"I know who took Camila."

CHAPTER SEVENTEEN

Vasquez was lost in thought, staring down at the file in front of him when a knock sounded at his door. He checked his watch and saw that his visitor was right on time. Vasquez didn't stand for delays. It was part of the reason why he could stomach working with Goddard. He was an arrogant son of a bitch, but when the guy made a plan, he stuck to it. But that wasn't going to last forever.

"Come in."

Vasquez was looking forward to good news. His plans had hit a complication, which was something else he didn't stand for. Complications caused problems, and Vasquez didn't need any more of those on his plate. He wanted a simplified life, one that allowed him to spend time with his family as well as provide for them. At the moment, he was only able to do the latter. That was going to change.

When Vasquez looked up at his visitor, he instantly knew he wasn't going to get the good news he was looking for. He flipped the folder shut and clasped his hands in front of him, following the movements of the mousy man who sat down on the edge of the chair opposite his boss. He clutched a briefcase to his chest.

Bartholomew Peters was an interesting man. He was an American, but unlike Vasquez, he did not seem built for the career he had chosen. Peters was good at numbers and faces. Those talents combined meant he could balance your books and remember every person you ever did business with. He was like Vasquez's very own personal computer. He was an incredible asset, as long as you didn't mind his quirks.

Since he was useful to him, Vasquez had learned to look past Peter's twitchy nature.

"Good morning, Bartholomew."

Peters just nodded. His eyes darted from Vasquez, to the window, to the desk, and back again. They moved in time with the ticking of the clock on the wall. He was in constant motion. Vasquez would've believed he was constantly strung out if he didn't know any better. That was another reason why he liked the man—he was boring. He had no interest in moving up or double crossing or gaining recognition. He was humble, simple, and predictable.

He was also trustworthy. Vasquez had earned Peters' loyalty over a decade ago, and in the time since, the former police lieutenant had never needed to call into question who Peters answered to. When he wasn't working for Vasquez, the tiny, thin-framed man was at home with his mother, watching black and white movies and putting together model airplanes.

It made little sense to Vasquez, but he had never been bothered enough to ask Peters why this was the life he had chosen. Peters was good at it, and that was enough for Vasquez.

"There's been a complication." His voice trembled less from fear and more from his constant movements. His right hand was tapping against the arm of his chair while both his legs bounced up and down in a rhythm only he found comforting.

"Explain." Vasquez had found the easiest way to deal with Peters was to be direct. The other man didn't particularly like social interaction, but Vasquez felt no loss at having to skip the small talk.

"A girl has been taken." He opened his briefcase and placed a picture of a young girl with light brown hair on Vasquez's desk. She looked like she could be about the same age as his granddaughter. Her smile was bright and her eyes were wide with innocence.

"Who is she?"

"Camila Torres, daughter of Javier Torres." Another picture landed on Vasquez's desk. The man looked familiar, but he couldn't quite place him.

"He's proven difficult in the past," Peters explained. "The job with Eriksson is the most memorable."

Vasquez shook his head. His relationship with his Swedish contacts was still rocky. "He works with Frank Skinner."

"From time to time."

"What does his daughter have to do with this?" Vasquez picked up her picture again, studying her face. She was beautiful. Her image made him miss his granddaughter.

"A video was delivered to Torres, warning him to back away from Goddard or else she would be killed."

"So our friend Jack Noble had no other choice than to fall in line."

Learning Noble's true identity had been mere luck, thanks to Peters' steel trap of a mind. One look at his picture, and the small man had dug through his files until he'd found the only scrap of information on him there was. It was a single name—Frank Skinner. Finding out more about Noble hadn't been easy, but Vasquez's network was extensive. He persisted and in the end it had paid off. He doubted he had Noble's full story, but it was enough to move him around the chess board as Vasquez saw fit.

Peters was silent, so Vasquez picked up the conversation again. "Do we know who has her?"

The other man shook his head.

Vasquez didn't want any harm to come to the girl. She was innocent and didn't deserve to pay for Goddard's mistakes. But just thinking about the senator made Vasquez's blood pressure rise. He had been dealing with Goddard for some time without consequence.

The man was arrogant, surely, but he was efficient. He was reliable. So few men were as predictable as the senator, and that was something Vasquez could use to his advantage.

But the man had threatened his family. Not directly, of course, but the message had been loud and clear. He had inquired after Vasquez's family, had even been so kind as to send his granddaughter a present. But in this business, that was not an act of kindness. It was a warning. *Do your job, or else. I know where your family is. I can get to them.*

That was unacceptable. Goddard might have a solid hand, but Vasquez had an ace up his sleeve in Jack Noble. He would do whatever was necessary to end Goddard so the man could never even think about coming after his family again. It would be regrettable if an innocent girl ended up in the crossfire, but as far as Vasquez was concerned, he had to take care of his own first and foremost.

"What about Michelle Hernandez?" Vasquez asked, slipping the two pictures on the table into his folder containing all the information they had on Jack Noble.

"I couldn't confirm her story about going to college with Jack Noble."

"Do you think she's lying?"

The other man twitched. He worked in facts, not opinions or informed guesses.

Vasquez sighed and let it go. He had other advisors who would be much more willing to have his ear. "It's likely she doesn't know who her old friend is these days. But she is of no consequence. She may even be useful to us. Goddard cares for her, trusts her. But she's involved with Nicolás Garcia right under his nose. We might be able to turn her, and if not, we might be able to use her as bait."

Peters didn't say anything else. Vasquez could tell he was reaching the end of his rope here. He had delivered all the information he had, and now it was time to return to his comfort zone at home with his mother and his movies and his models.

"Thank you, Bartholomew." Vasquez stood but didn't extend his hand. He almost laughed at the entire situation. If anyone else acted the way Peters did, Vasquez would quickly put them in their place. Peters, luckily for him, was the exception. His assets were worth the inconveniences.

Peters clutched his briefcase to his chest and shuffled from the room. As the door swung shut, Vasquez called for the man stationed outside his office. Aguilar caught the door and popped his head inside. Vasquez waved him in.

"I need to know who took this girl." Vasquez pulled the picture of Javier's daughter out of the folder and handed it to his man. "Her name is Camila Torres."

Aguilar's gaze swept over the girl's face before looking back up at his boss. "Right away."

Vasquez dismissed him, knowing they'd find something eventually. He could do the work himself, and probably in less time, but he had bigger matters to worry about. Vasquez flipped the folder back open and turned to Jack Noble's dossier. He was an impressive man, as was his associate, Riley Logan. The pair of them could take out Goddard much more easily than Vasquez, with the added benefit of Vasquez not appearing to have anything to do with the senator's death.

Vasquez didn't want Goddard's empire, but he couldn't deny that having that sort of power would add extra protection for his family. No one would ever think of threatening them again.

On the other hand, it would extend Vasquez's circle of enemies. That sort of power also came with a larger target on your back, as Goddard would soon find out.

CHAPTER EIGHTEEN

Jack wouldn't tell us who took Camila until we were all gathered at the compound. Javier had returned from giving Marianna's family the terrible news. His eyes were rimmed red and his mouth was set in a hard line. It couldn't have been easy to relay that information, let alone do it knowing that his daughter could be the next victim.

Jack had to suppress his excitement in the face of Javier's grief. I could tell it was difficult for him. He'd been upbeat since his revelation in the car. It was starting to get on my damn nerves.

We were gathered in Javier's office. Sadie and I took the comfortable chairs while Javier sat behind his desk. Jack paced the room behind us. It made the hair on the back of my neck stand on end.

"Will you get on with it, man?" I said.

Jack stopped short between the chairs and the desk, then turned to Javier. "I know who took Camila."

Javier lurched up, causing his entire desk to shift. A look of wild hope and panic crossed his face. "Who? Who took her?"

"Nicolás Garcia."

All three of our heads whipped around to look at Jack. Sadie had an incredulous look on her face. "How the hell did you come to that conclusion?"

"Something he said rubbed me the wrong way. When he was talking to Sadie, he said Goddard was useful—for now. He said Goddard would have to stay in the picture until he could find a way to *remove him himself.* If he found out about the hit on Goddard, if he knew Javier was involved, the only way to guarantee nothing happened until the time was right would be to kidnap Camila."

Javier stood stone still behind his desk. "I'm going to kill that bastard myself."

"Wait just a second," I said, holding up my hands. I had to walk a fine line here. Javier would want to move as quickly as possible, but if we played this wrong, it wouldn't just be Camila who might end up on the wrong side of the barrel.

"I'm not waiting another goddamn minute, Bear. This is my daughter."

"I know, but we can't rush this. We can't risk it going sideways. Just hear me out." I waited until Javier slumped back into his chair before I continued. "Jack, how sure are you it's Nicolás?"

"It makes sense," Sadie said.

Jack started pacing again. "The man's making moves. He's playing a big game right now. Unless there's someone else in play we haven't even come up against, I don't see who else it could be. Goddard would've just taken me out. He wouldn't have gone to the trouble of taking the girl if all he wanted was for the hit to be called off. Nicolás is biding his time. And doesn't it seem odd that Goddard hasn't mentioned it? Why? Because he doesn't know. His benefactor doesn't want him to know."

"Which means what for my daughter?"

I looked at Javier. "It could be good news."

"She's being held captive by the current leader of a drug cartel. Explain to me, exactly, how that's good news."

"Nicolás doesn't want to kill Camila—"

"He already killed an innocent girl."

"Yes, but not Camila," I said. "She has more value to him than Marianna did."

Sadie turned toward me. "You're a bastard."

I took a deep breath before I answered her. Rising tempers wouldn't solve any of our problems. "I'm speaking from Nicolás's point of view. We have to keep some objectivity here. In his mind, Marianna was nobody. She served a single purpose—to send a message. Camila is collateral. He wants Goddard dead, but he wants him dead on his terms. He'll hold onto Camila until the time is right to set things in motion."

"You don't think he'd hurt her?" Sadie sounded skeptical.

I looked to Jack, who nodded. He knew where I was going with this. Perks of having worked together for so long. Sometimes we could read each other's minds. "No, I don't. Not unless he's pushed to that point."

"I can't take that risk," Javier said.

I nodded. I wasn't unsympathetic to his situation. "All I'm saying is we may have a little more time to work with than we thought. We have a pretty good idea of who took her—"

"I know it was him," Jack said. "I know it was."

I tipped my head in his direction. "We know Nicolás took her, then. That will help us narrow down where she's being kept. He won't hurt her, not as long as he feels he's in control."

"And how do we make sure he feels like he stays in control?" Sadie asked.

I rubbed at my jaw. "He knows Javier is involved in the hit being taken out on Goddard, but he doesn't know about me or Jack."

Javier sat up straighter in his chair. "How do you figure?"

My gaze slid over to Sadie. "What's your involvement with him?"

She looked angry. "Excuse me?"

"He loves you."

"He's a bastard."

"Then he's a bastard who loves you."

"I've had to play my part for a while now. I'm convincing."

I couldn't quite read the expression on Jack's face when he asked, "Did you get caught up?"

Sadie opened her mouth to give him a heated reply, but apparently thought better of it. She closed her eyes, took a deep breath, and looked up at Jack calmly. "It can be difficult to separate Michelle from Sadie sometimes. There was a moment where I thought I could change him, where I thought he could be an ally. But I underestimated his thirst for power. I haven't made that mistake again."

Jack looked back at her gravely. "I understand."

Sadie turned back to me. "He and Michelle are involved. A few people know about it. His uncle found out, but kept his mouth shut. He always liked me. Goddard doesn't know."

"You're sure about that?"

"Absolutely." She crossed one leg over the other. "Goddard trusts me more than he trusts most. He cares about me like a daughter. If he knew I was involved with Nicolás, he would not be happy. He never liked Mateo's nephew. He's too much of a hothead. Too unreliable."

"I'd like to know where Nicolás got his information." Jack turned to Javier. "Have you talked to your men yet?"

"I've got someone I trust asking questions. Discreetly. If there's a leak, he'll likely find it. But I'm not holding my breath."

"I don't think he got the information from here. Or, if he did, someone is still holding out on him. Someone is trying to control Nicolás as much as Nicolás is trying to control Javier."

I twisted in my seat to face Sadie again. "If Nicolás had any idea Jack was involved with Javier's operation, he would've taken him out the second Jack stepped across his threshold. He's in love with you, and if he knew Jack wasn't who he said he was, then he'd put a bullet in his brain as soon as look at him. All in the name of protecting you."

Sadie rubbed at her forehead. "That's a definite possibility."

Javier leaned forward on his desk, palms flat against its surface. I could see the tension running through his body. "What does this all mean for my Camila?"

I leaned forward, placing my elbows on my knees. "Nicolás has

Camila in the hopes of getting you to back off on the hit until he decides it's the right time to take him out. In the meantime, he won't hurt her and risk losing his leverage."

Sadie scoffed. "That doesn't mean another girl won't show up dead."

"Fair point. We can't risk waiting too long, but we've got some time to work with. We just have to figure out what to do with it."

"My men are still looking into the origins of the video," Javier said. "Once they find it, we'll know where she's being held."

Jack crossed his arms over his chest. "It'll be a start. Just because she was taken there for the video doesn't mean she's being kept there. But it'll get us one step closer."

Javier worked his jaw back and forth. It couldn't be easy to just sit and wait for something to happen with his daughter's life on the line.

"In the meantime," I said, "we need to figure out what Nicolás is up to and make sure Goddard agrees to leave him alone. If the senator doesn't stay in his lane, there's a chance he could put a hit out on Nicolás and Camila may end up being in the wind."

Or dead, I thought. I didn't feel like it needed to be said, even though the scenario was clear to all four of us.

"One good thing we have going for us," Jack said, "is I think Goddard is interested in testing my skills, which means he may be calling us to do the deed. It'll at least give us a heads up on his plans."

A buzzing sounded somewhere in the room, and all four of us reached into our pockets for our phones. Sadie was the one who fished hers out first, the screen lighting up in her hand. She turned it to show the rest of us. Goddard's name was clear on the display.

"Speak of the devil."

CHAPTER NINETEEN

S adie stood up and crossed to the back. We were all holding our breaths. Goddard had no reason to suspect she wasn't who she said she was, but there was always that risk he had uncovered a piece of information that led to that conclusion. We weren't about to add to that risk by opening our mouths.

Sadie answered the phone in her soft accent. "Thomas."

We couldn't hear Goddard's replies, but a lot could be said for how Sadie's body tensed and relaxed in response to his words. It said something for the comfort she felt to be in a room with us that she didn't feel the need to hide her reactions to what the senator was saying.

"Yes, of course." She paused. "When? All right. No, that's not a problem. I'll give him a call. As far as I know he doesn't have anything going on right now."

A small smile spread over her face as she turned to look at Jack. "Yes, he's aware. I'm not worried about him. He's been good to me over the years. He knows what will happen to him if he ever breaks my heart."

I turned to Jack, who had a smirk on his face. I knew nothing was going on between the two of them—it's not like they'd had time to talk about it anyway—but after the initial shock of Sadie's true identity had worn off, it seemed as though things were going back to the cautious flirtations they had been passing between each other prior to that little revelation.

"Of course," Sadie said. "I'll see you later. Bye."

I watched as Sadie pocketed her phone, the smile slowly replaced by a much more serious look. I had a guess as to what the phone call was about. "He wants to see what Jack can do."

Sadie nodded. "He didn't say as much, but that's what it sounds like to me. He wants to meet us this afternoon. He wants me to tell Jack he's got a job ready for him."

"And you didn't inquire as to what that was?"

"There was no point, not over the phone. Goddard trusts me, likes me even, but he doesn't stand to be questioned. We'd do better to confront him face to face if he's thinking about going after Nicolás. We need to read the situation, look at the playing field, and try to convince him it won't be worth the fallout."

I leaned back in my chair. "I thought you had convinced him to keep Nicolás in play for as long as possible?"

"Something else must have happened," she said. "Or someone else had gotten in his ear. My opinion means something, but he doesn't know me as a tactician. I work with the numbers. He'd ask his advisors, he'd go to Vasquez, and ask them what they thought was best."

"Whoever has his ear could be interested in taking Nicolás out so they can step into his place. Goddard will need to find a replacement if he goes through with this."

Javier stood up. "Whoever has his ear could also be interested in upping the timeline with Camila. Making us take Nicolás out would mean we'd have to find her sooner rather than later, also allowing us to perform the hit on Goddard. This person could be playing Goddard more than he realizes."

"It's definitely a possibility." Jack paused, and then eyed me. "You should be there, big man."

I blinked up at him. "What?"

Sadie echoed my sentiments. Javier looked on, his eyebrows knit together.

"We're walking a fine line here. There are a lot of moving parts, and a lot of people's lives on the line. If we mess this up, we're gonna need you."

"I'll be close by—"

"And how much will that help us if bullets start flying?"

"But they've already spotted Bear," Javier said. "If we introduce him into play now, they're going to be suspicious of him, not to mention of you and Sadie. It could blow up in our faces. I won't put my daughter's life on the line like this."

A beat of silence was passed around the room.

"It's not a bad idea." We all twisted around to look at her as soon as the words left Sadie's mouth.

"How can you say that, knowing Camila's life is hanging by a thread? Knowing that your cover could be blown if we make one wrong move?"

Sadie moved across the room, passed by Jack, and stood next to Javier. She had a genuine look of compassion on her face. "This thing is going to end one way or another. My gig is up now. We rescue Camila and we take out Goddard. We need to start making moves before Goddard does, or we're going to be left with a gun to our heads."

I stood up and walked over to stand on the other side of Javier's desk. Jack joined us. "But they know who I am. They spotted me that first night."

"I can tell them you're my man. Had you see what Michelle was up to. Tell them you messed up."

I flipped him off and he grinned, but it fell from his face quickly enough.

Sadie turned back to Javier. "Having one more guy on the inside gives us a greater advantage."

Javier closed his eyes and leaned forward on his desk with closed fists. A couple knuckles popped. "All right. Let's do this."

———

MICHELLE DROVE HER CAR OVER TO GODDARD'S HOUSE. IT WAS forty minutes or so outside the city. A place not many people knew of, and even fewer knew Goddard owned it. Jack rode shotgun, while I sat behind her in the back. Her Camry was nice, but it wasn't meant for a man as big as I was. If I had tried to sit behind Jack, I would've felt trapped. As it was, I wasn't too comfortable with my knees pressed up against the back of her seat, despite the fact she had moved up as far as she could.

Jack twisted around to look back at me. "Duck down, Bear. We don't want them to notice you too soon."

"Screw you, man."

Jack laughed and I even saw that Sadie cracked a smile in the rearview mirror. The air in the car remained heavy with anticipation. This was a risk and we all knew it. As soon as the front gate to Goddard's mansion came into view we turned serious. They'd spot me as soon as we passed through, and the senator's men would be all over us once we pulled up to the house.

Sadie rolled down her window and punched in the entry code that would open the gate. I leaned away from the window so the camera wouldn't catch my face. They'd know a third person was in the car with her, but if they didn't have a clue it was me, it would buy us a little time to explain the situation.

As the gate slid open, Sadie looked in the rearview and caught my eye. "Ready?"

"As I'll ever be." My heart was steady, but the burn of adrenaline pumping through my veins warmed my muscles. With any luck this would be the only big risk we took today. But luck hadn't been on our side lately.

Had it ever been?

Sadie pulled through the gate and made her way down the long drive. It was lined with tall manicured trees and opened to a sprawling lawn at the final bend. Several soldiers were waiting on the front steps with their rifles raised. There were six of them in view, and potentially more that we couldn't see.

"Go easy," Jack said. "Let's not give them an excuse."

Sadie gripped the wheel as she pulled forward. I saw her face transform as she slipped into Michelle's persona. She seemed to shrink a little in her seat, looking softer and more concerned. She really was a chameleon.

Spero was standing back from his men, his two-tone pistol hanging at his side. I noticed the suppressor threaded to the barrel. As far as he was concerned, he was in complete control with his guys armed and locked onto us. He looked calm and collected as he shouted at the detail. Then he approached us.

"Out of the car."

Sadie looked at Jack, who shrugged his shoulders. The three of us opened our doors in unison and stepped out with our hands in plain view. My pulse quickened. Tended to happen when half a dozen semi-automatic weapons were pointed in your general direction. Sadie had convinced us to leave our firearms in the car. I was itching to grab for the Springfield but that would end with all three of us face down in the driveway, swimming in pools of our own blood.

The door opened and Goddard stepped out behind Spero. He looked at me for a moment, then his gaze shifted to Jack, and finally settled on Sadie. "What the hell is going on?"

Sadie took a meek step forward. The guns trained on her sharpened their focus. She swallowed hard, cleared her throat. "I can explain."

CHAPTER TWENTY

G oddard walked down the stairs leading to the front of the house and met Spero. Small lights set in the concrete stairs illuminated his path. A breeze came in from the east carrying with it a hint of freshly cut grass. The smell was sweet and lingered in the back of my throat.

Spero said, "Explain quickly or my men will be instructed to find a place to bury three corpses."

Goddard gave Spero a sharp look but didn't say anything. He trusted Sadie, but Spero was paid to keep him safe. The man was just doing his job and Sadie had given them plenty of reason to proceed with caution. Goddard took great lengths to keep anyone from knowing about the residence. Hell, he'd bought the place with blood money. You didn't just show up unannounced.

"Thomas." Sadie's voice quivered. "Can you tell them to lower the guns, please?"

Goddard took a moment to think it over. He gestured at me and Jack. "Are they armed?"

Sadie shook her head. "I told them to keep their guns in the car. They're not looking for a fight. They want to help."

Spero kept his finger aimed at me. "This man was seen lurking around Café Flores the other day. It's quite a coincidence that he's here now, no?"

"I can explain that." Jack took a step forward, and two of the guns narrowed in on him. He kept his hands in view and held his ground. He looked concerned on the surface, but this was all a game to him. Look like you were afraid and it made the other person feel complacent. "He's my guy."

Spero spit on the ground then said, "I have no reason to trust you. Or your man."

"I vouched for Jack," Sadie said. "You had him vetted. He's clean."

He gestured with his sidearm. "Doesn't mean this guy is."

Goddard glanced at his watch then looked around the property. "The courtesy of your word extended to Jack, Michelle. It does not extend to his friends, too."

Sadie lowered her gaze. "I'm sorry. I guess I wasn't thinking of..."

The senator looked to the sky as if it would give him guidance. "Jack? You have anything to say? Can you clue me in on why someone with your credentials would do something so damn stupid?"

"His name's Riley," Jack said. "We go way back. And we're as good of a team as you'll find this side of the Atlantic. As much as I hate to admit it, he's a better shot than me. Better tactician than me, too. When I'm impatient, he reels me in. I thought those skills might come in handy."

Spero gestured in my direction, this time without his pistol. "And why was he outside the café the other day?"

Jack nodded and had a half grin on his face that made him look sheepish. "That was my bad. I had spotted Michelle earlier in the day. Almost didn't recognize her. She's changed a lot since college."

Sadie glanced at Jack but averted her eyes just as quickly. She couldn't show surprise to anything he said.

Jack continued. "In this line of business you rarely run into old friends out of coincidence. I'm sure you know what I mean, Senator. I had Riley check her out. See what she was up to."

"She wasn't there that morning at the café." Spiro tightened his grip on his firearm.

"I'd been following her for a day or two. Noticed she'd met up with Senator Goddard a couple of times. I was interested to see what kind of person he was."

Goddard took a few steps forward, placing himself between his security detail and us. "That's highly convenient, Mr. Smith."

Jack shrugged. "Like I said, I rarely run into old friends out of coincidence. But it happens every once in a while. I didn't even know who you were before she told me that night at the restaurant. I don't make a habit of following politics. Gives me indigestion."

Goddard and Spero both looked over at Sadie, who nodded to confirm Jack's story. It was a matter of how much they truly trusted her. After a few tense seconds, Spero diverted his gaze toward me. Looked like he was sizing me up.

"Maybe you should stick with taking the shots instead of tailing the targets. Don't know if you are aware of this but you kinda stick out."

I tossed a glance at Jack. "So I've been told."

Goddard continued to stare at Sadie. A tear slipped down her cheek and she moved to wipe it away. He addressed the men in front of him. "Lower your weapons."

"Sir." Spero turned on his heel toward his boss. "I don't advise—"

Goddard silenced his security chief with a slice of his hand. "I said lower your weapons."

The men looked to Spero, who nodded. They were his guys. The senator was second in command in their eyes. Spero's lips thinned to the point of disappearing and his jaw was clenched so tight the muscles at the corner rippled and I thought he might snap a tooth or two in half.

"Spero, take Franklin and escort our guests to my office."

Goddard's narrow stare was now fixed on me. "I'll be with them momentarily."

Spero looked like he wanted to say more, but he was forced to swallow his words as Goddard disappeared back into the house. The door stood open after he slipped out of view. When Spero turned back to us he had his eyes on me. I offered him nothing but a dead stare. The boss had spoken. There was nothing he could do about it no matter how much he wanted to.

Spero's men cleared out in teams of two. Franklin led us into the house. A cold blast of air scented like flowers blew down from a wide vent over the door. Beyond that I detected a hint of seared animal flesh. A pan rattled on the stove and a knife slapped on a cutting board somewhere beyond the entryway.

We were led up the stairs and into a wide foyer adorned with a couch and a couple chairs and a tall bookcase. Every tome on its shelves looked a hundred years old. Worn and weathered spines faced outward, the lettering faded. A dark wooden staircase led up to the second floor, but we bypassed it in favor of a narrow hallway. Spero stayed close enough to me that I felt his hot breath on my neck. I turned around and gave him a smile. He shoved me forward and I just chuckled. It was too easy to get under his skin. If I kept it up, I might rattle him enough that he'd give something up.

We entered an office with walls made of dark mahogany. It had high ceilings, tall windows, and extensive book cases. Looked like a law library. Jack and Sadie took the sofa and I plopped myself in a leather chair that practically swallowed me whole. Not an easy feat for a piece of furniture. I leaned back and folded my hands in my lap and closed my eyes. The more relaxed I looked the less suspicious it made me and the more it bothered Spero. It was win-win all around.

A few minutes passed with only the sound of a ticking grandfather clock before Goddard entered the room. He had removed his jacket and rolled up his sleeves. His tie was open to the middle of his chest, his shirt unbuttoned almost as far. His hair stood at odd angles.

I hadn't seen him this disheveled before. Didn't know it was possible. Had we thrown him a curveball, or was it something else?

The senator turned to his men. "Wait outside."

Spero held up his hand. "Sir—"

"Now."

Spero clenched his jaw again, but nodded like a good soldier. He looked over at Jack and then at me. I gave him a two-fingered salute. He left the room ahead of Franklin who followed behind a second later.

"You really shouldn't push Spero." Goddard slid into his chair. It was large and overbearing and made him a head higher than anyone else seated in the room. "He has a temper."

I shrugged my shoulders. "I only do it because it's so easy."

Goddard chuckled, but I could see the calculating look in his eyes. He turned his gaze on Sadie. "That could've ended badly for you out there."

She leaned forward on the sofa, forearms crossed, fingers dangling toward the floor. "I see that now. I'm sorry, Thomas. I just wasn't thinking. I wanted to help."

Goddard clasped his hands behind his head and leaned back. His chair groaned as it tipped a few inches away from the desk. He looked more comfortable now, but a vein still twitched at his temple in time with his heartbeat. His ability to go with the flow and work under pressure was what had advanced him so far in the world of politics. I'd almost be impressed, if I wasn't looking forward to putting a gun to his head and pulling the trigger.

He stared at a spot on the wall above us. "And how do you expect your friends to help?"

Sadie shifted and bit her bottom lip. She was about to say something risky. "You've decided to take out Nicolás after all."

Goddard didn't react on the surface, but the minor hesitation before he spoke was enough to indicate he hadn't expected her to guess that much. "What makes you say that?"

"What he did was unacceptable. He's not staying in his lane.

Even if he were a better leader than Mateo, which he's not, he put your operation at risk."

A smile spread over Goddard's face. "You pay attention." He grew serious. "You've been close to Nicolás in the past."

Sadie shifted uncomfortably. Was that what Michelle would do? Or was it a genuine reaction? "You knew about that?"

"I know everything, Michelle."

My heart skipped a beat. *Hopefully not everything.*

"He was good to me once." Sadie's voice caught. This one I was certain was genuine. "But I never wanted him to do this. I never wanted him to lead his uncle's business."

"Do I have to worry about your feelings getting in the way of what needs to happen?" Goddard was turning colder. His icy stare revealed the killer inside. Javier had warned us—even when the senator didn't pull the trigger himself, he was usually the one who ordered the hit.

Sadie sat up on the couch and looked Goddard dead in the eye. "No."

"And how do I know that? You've already surprised me once today."

"You can trust me, Thomas." Sadie didn't give anything away as she spoke. "Nicolás meant something to me once before, but I learned a while ago I couldn't rely on him. Not like I could rely on you."

Goddard held her gaze for several seconds before his eyebrows unknit, his eyes relaxed, his tight lips parted and spread. He took a deep breath then nodded. She had him wrapped around her finger.

There was a beat of silence, and Jack couldn't let it go on for a second longer than was comfortable. He leaned forward. "So what now?"

Goddard looked between me and Jack, then he leaned back in his chair again and kicked his feet up on his desk. A smile spread across his face. "Now you tell me how you're going to kill Nicolás Garcia."

CHAPTER TWENTY-ONE

I met Jack's gaze with an eyebrow raised. This was what we came here to do. We were walking on thin ice as it was testing the limits of Goddard's trust. Now we had to deliver. Sadie wouldn't be much help in this situation. She *couldn't* be. The senator didn't know the kind of tactical brain she had, and we couldn't risk revealing that side of her. It'd blow her cover and spell the end of the three of us. Jack had Goddard's trust more than I did, so he would have to lead the conversation. I'd have to prove my worth.

Jack crossed an ankle over a knee. "I'd recommend hitting him at his house. I've already been there. I haven't seen the whole thing, but I'm more familiar with it than anywhere else we could meet up with him."

"It'll put him at ease, too," I said. "If he's as arrogant and hotheaded as I've heard, he'll be cocky inside his own house. We can use that to our advantage."

Goddard's attention cut to me for a moment but slid back over to Jack. My words had been noted out of courtesy. I tried to let the dismissal bounce away by imagining what it would feel like for my fist to connect to his face.

Jack acknowledged my input with a tip of his head. "He won't imagine we'd take a risk like that on his turf."

"How would you get an invite?" Goddard said. "He doesn't know you. I imagine he trusts you even less than I do."

Jack turned to Sadie and gave her a questioning look.

Goddard's feet slid off the desk and slammed onto the floor. His body jerked upright. "No."

"She's our only way in."

"I will not allow you to put Michelle in danger like that. It is out of the question."

Sadie said, "Thomas—"

"No."

"Thomas." Sadie's voice was quiet but authoritative. "I know I can get us back in there."

"You'll be killed."

"I'll take care of her." Jack gestured at me, his eyes focused on Goddard. "We both will."

"You'll understand that I don't trust you have her best interests at heart."

Jack's head cocked to the side. "And you'll understand that I've known this girl for half my life. We may not have stayed in touch that entire time, but I've cared about her for much longer than you have."

"Jack." Sadie laid a calming hand on his arm and looked up at Goddard.

The senator's lips disappeared after he licked them. He took a deep breath through his nose then steepled his hands in front of his face. His eyes shut for a few seconds. Then his face relaxed. He'd made his decision. "Understand this. If anything happens to her there will be no country, no island, no iceberg where you can hide from my vengeance. You might as well turn your pistols on yourselves because I can guarantee I will not show an ounce of mercy. When I'm through with you, your dead grandmothers will wail from the grave begging me to finally kill you."

"If anything happens to her," Jack said, "I won't even try."

Goddard turned back to Sadie. "What will be your reason for calling on Nicolás?"

Sadie looked away. "Nicolás and I have maintained some semblance of a relationship."

"Did you know he was going to move against his uncle?" There was an eerie calm to the senator's voice.

"No." Sadie chose her words carefully. "He had talked about it before, but it felt like all bluster to me. He loved his uncle, even if they didn't always see eye to eye. I didn't think he could ever be capable of this."

"Why didn't you come to me with that information?"

"I just didn't deem it newsworthy."

"And now that you know? What does it change?"

Sadie bowed her head. "Everything. I can't trust him. He is no longer the person I thought he was."

"We are not good people, Michelle." The senator looked fatherly as he watched her, but there was a coldness to his voice that was unsettling. "You should know that by now."

"But there's goodness in you. In all of us." She took a deep, shuddering breath. "I've done my fair share of terrible things. I'm not innocent here either, but if he can turn against Mateo, who says he won't turn against you? I wouldn't know what to do with myself."

"You would be taken care of." Goddard turned to Jack. "You advised me to keep him alive earlier. What's changed?"

Jack shrugged. "Honestly, I don't care. I'm helping out a friend. It's good karma."

"Is that all it is?"

"And a good paycheck." He paused a beat. "But I have to know that once we take out Nicolás, we're not held responsible for the fallout."

"You do this job, you get paid, you leave," Goddard said. "I don't need your career choices to affect Michelle. Or me, for that matter."

"Thomas," Sadie started.

He held up a hand. "It's non-negotiable. You can have your goodbyes, and then I don't ever want to see you again, Jack. Or your friend."

I laughed. "Not a problem for me, man."

Jack worked his jaw, but nodded. He turned to Sadie. "He's got a point. I'm not the man you knew back then. Being friends with me comes with consequences."

Jack may have been following a script, but the lines rang true nonetheless. We'd both been through plenty to feel that way, and I could tell Jack meant the words either way.

I clapped my hands in an attempt to break the moment. "All right. So when do we get started?" My stomach growled audibly. "And does this job come with a complimentary lunch?"

GODDARD ORDERED HIS CHEF TO PREPARE US FOOD. THE MAN pulled a slab of beef from the fridge and went to work carving it. Smoke rose over the cooktop as the meat sizzled. The smell overtook the room.

We gathered around the dining room table with maps of Nicolás's house and information on the movements of his men. In the last twenty-four hours he had doubled his force. He was paranoid that someone would make a move against him—whether that was Goddard, another cartel looking to move in while chaos reigned, or somebody within his ranks.

Goddard watched without input as Jack and I planned our hit. The idea was to have Sadie get Jack in the door again. He'd deal with Nicolás and his men on the inside. I would make my way around the outside of the compound and systematically take out his guards. They were heavily armed, but if they were anything like that kid in the forest, their training was subpar. We didn't think there'd be much of a fight as long as we kept the element of surprise.

Sadie returned to the table after having a hushed conversation over the phone with Nicolás on the back deck. She left the French doors open and a steady breeze blew in. The humidity had dissipated after a quick thunderstorm, leaving the air cool and refreshing.

"He's agreed to meet with me," she said.

"Does he know I'll be there too?" Jack asked.

She nodded. "He doesn't like that you're my new bodyguard. He wishes it was one of his guys, but I told him I trust you with my life. For now that seems to be enough."

Goddard was peeling an orange, looking unconcerned. He wasn't one for doing the actual planning, but he wanted to supervise our every move. Jack and I ignored him the best we could. He put his knife down and began to piece out the sections of the fruit. "What did you tell him?"

"I told him you were looking to put a hit out on him."

Goddard looked up sharply. This would be met with repercussions if things didn't work out the way we planned. "And what happened to needing the element of surprise?"

"We need a valid excuse to meet there. He didn't think it was safe for us to talk right now in case you were watching him. I had to make it clear this needed to happen sooner rather than later."

Jack straightened up and stretched his back. We'd been bending over these maps for the last half-hour or so. "He'll never think we're the ones there to do the job. Between Sadie's presence and giving him the heads up, he'll be relaxed."

The senator tapped one of the maps. "He's doubled his men. That's not exactly relaxed."

It looked like Goddard was about to change his mind about sending Sadie in, so I interjected. "Trust me, he's not going to see this coming. He's blinded by Michelle's presence. It's the best plan we've got, and we don't have time to come up with a better one. We need her to get Jack inside."

"Fine." Goddard grabbed a napkin and wiped his hands. "But I'm sending a few of my men along with you."

Jack and I tensed at the same time. More men meant more confusion and more restraints we had to operate under. That wasn't ideal. Jack spoke first.

"No offense, Senator, but I don't trust your men."

"And I don't trust you." Goddard stood up. "At least we're on an even playing field."

"And how do we know your guys will give us the room we need? Your man Spero wasn't too happy to see us earlier."

"Spero will fall in line." He looked over at me. "He'll be there to make sure you're able to take out the guards on the outside."

I ground my teeth together. "I've been in worse scrapes before. I don't need the help."

"Forgive me, but I don't really give a rat's ass what you think you can or cannot do. You want the job? You want the money? You want your life? You'll do this my way."

We all exchanged a look. We knew Goddard would want to send a few of his men along to keep an eye on us. It was another element in play that we didn't need to make an already complicated op even more so, but what choice did we have? We had to get inside and get to Nicolás before he decided Camila wasn't worth the trouble anymore.

Jack leaned forward across the table with his hand extended. "Deal."

CHAPTER TWENTY-TWO

March 27, 2006

Sadie and Jack pulled up to Nicolás's house after a long and silent car ride. It was eight a.m. and already eight-five degrees out and the air conditioning in Sadie's vehicle worked half-ass at best. Sweat trickled down Jack's face, his neck, and settled in his shirt collar. He didn't care. It'd been twenty-four hours since he'd showered. A little sweat wasn't going to make much of a difference.

Jack had vetoed either of them going in with comms on. It meant Bear would be as much in the dark as Goddard was. At least they'd be able to play out this Nicolás situation without having to use doublespeak. Goddard hadn't liked the idea, but Jack convinced him that going in mic'd up wasn't a risk worth taking. In exchange, they'd agreed for the senator to send two extra men who would have mics on them. Bear would have to play it safe.

Sadie kept her foot on the brake, and her hand on the shifter, still in drive. She looked over at Jack. "Have I thanked you yet?"

He shrugged. "No. Do you feel like you need to?"

She gripped the wheel with both hands until her knuckles turned white, then relinquished her grasp and watched as the color returned.

"I didn't exactly walk into your life on the best of terms. You're risking a lot here."

Jack watched through the windshield as two of Nicolás's armed men made their way toward the car. "Didn't have much choice. But even if I had I'm not that much of a bastard that I'd let an innocent girl die. Or risk the life of an agent, even one from the CIA."

She laughed. "How sweet."

Jack knew it wasn't the answer she had been looking for. He felt himself being pulled toward her and had a feeling Sadie felt it too. But what he had said earlier in Goddard's office was true—being friends with him came with consequences. She was with the Agency. Jack could never live a life like that again. It would be better if they continued circling each other without closing the gap and then move on with their lives. When he left Costa Rica, he'd leave her behind. It was best for both of them.

Before either could say anything else one of Nicolás's men tapped on Jack's window. Jack showed his hands and Sadie followed suit after cutting the engine. Both their doors were opened for them. They got out of the car and endured a pat down. The man searching Jack found the Glock. He pulled it from Jack's waistband and gave him a look. Jack shrugged to say, *can you blame me?* The man dropped the magazine, ejected the chambered round, and tossed the gun in the front seat of the car then pushed Jack forward toward the house. He stumbled then caught his step and moved on.

As they walked up the stairs he glanced around the grounds. He knew Bear and Goddard's men were out there. Where, he wasn't sure. Half a dozen of Nicolás's men were visible around the outside of the house. There would also be guards in the woods and inside the house. They knew what to expect even if they didn't have an exact count.

As Jack crossed the threshold behind Sadie he started to count down. They'd have roughly five minutes to isolate Nicolás and put him at ease before Bear and the others started moving in. The goal for the men outside was to take Nicolas's men out quickly and systematically. No guns. No commotion. Jack and Sadie needed as much time as possible before the proverbial alarms started going off. As much as Jack didn't like the idea that Goddard had his own team here, they were going to be useful.

The two of them were ushered into the same room they had stood in before. The smell of burning tobacco met them as they entered. Nicolás was sitting on the sofa, cigar in hand, reading a newspaper. On the table next to him was a drink. Perhaps he was trying to look like his slain uncle. He appeared relaxed, but it was just a front. There were twice as many men in plain sight as there had been before and Nicolás's gun was visible on the table next to his drink.

Through the haze of cigar smoke Nicolás's gaze landed on Jack first. He looked him up and down before he switched over to Sadie. Jack could tell how much the man wanted her on his side, but just like last time he wasn't going to beg with his men around. He had a reputation to maintain, especially now that he'd proven he had the cajones to take out his own uncle.

"Michelle."

"Nicolás." There was a beat of silence while Sadie looked around the room, taking in the scene. "Do we have to talk in front of them?"

Nicolás jutted his chin to the side. He was being cautious, but it was a bluff. "If they go, so does he." He aimed his twisted index finger at Jack.

Jack smirked. "Come on, man. You still don't trust me? Look at this face."

"He tried to bring a weapon on the premises." The man who spoke was the same one who had felt Jack up outside of the car.

"It was for her protection. We both have the same goal here. You don't want anything to happen to her and neither do I."

Nicolás's gaze danced around the room. His men were trustworthy, sure. But not all these guys were his men. How many had been loyal to his uncle just two days ago? How much did they know of his relationship with his uncle's former accountant?

"If they go, so do you, gringo," Nicolás said.

He was playing right into their hands. "Fair enough." Jack turned toward the door. "What does a guy have to do to get a cup of coffee around here?"

Nicolás nodded at one of his men and the group led Jack out of the room, shutting the doors behind them.

"Seriously though," Jack said. "Can I get a cup of coffee?"

"Sit down and shut up." The man who spoke was the one that Jack suspected was Nicolás's personal bodyguard, the man who gave orders to the others. He was sharp, but his temper was short and Jack thought he could use that to his advantage. After all one of his best skills was getting under people's skin.

"Relax, bro. I'm outnumbered six to one. What are you worried about?" He patted his pockets like he was looking for something. This set the other men on edge. "You think your boss is going to appreciate us hanging out here, listening to their little lover's spat?" When the man didn't say anything else, Jack pushed harder. "Is this how you treat your guests?"

"We don't owe you shit."

Jack took a step forward and stood toe to toe with the man, who was at least a head shorter than him. "What's your name?"

The man didn't back down. "Goya."

"Well, Goya, I'm the guy who's going to keep your boss alive. What do you think's gonna happen when we take out Goddard and he lands on top? He's going to reward the guy that made it happen." He grabbed a pack of cigarettes from Goya's shirt pocket, fished one from the pack and held it between his thumb and index finger. "You see, that guy's me. And what do you think's gonna happen when I become his right hand man? I'm going to reward the guy who knew his place and pointed me in the direction of a goddamn cup of coffee." He looked at the cigarette. "And a lighter."

Goya looked away at one of his men and laughed. But his face gave him away. His shoulders tensed as he prepared to strike. Jack tightened his stomach as the other man drove an uppercut to his solar plexus. When the blow landed it didn't take the wind out of him, but he doubled over anyway. Jack needed to make the guy feel like he had gotten one over on him. His arrogance would be his downfall.

Goya bent down to speak in Jack's ear. His hot breath smelled of tortillas. "The second Goddard is out of the picture, so are you, asshole. Nicolás may trust you for now, but that's only going to last for so long. He rewards the men who have stood by him over the years. You'll have a long way to climb if you think you'll have his ear."

Jack gasped out a breath and straightened up slowly. He looked around. Each of the men standing there looked ready to take him down if he made the wrong move. He slapped a grimace on his face, and said, "Look, man, we're here for the same reason. We both want Goddard gone. We're both gonna benefit from it."

"Some more than others." Goya looked over Jack's shoulder and nodded at one of his men. He then gestured for Jack to turn and head down a narrow hallway.

"Clear out," Goya shouted at a couple of workers who were preparing breakfast for the household. They scampered out of the way without having to be told twice.

Jack spotted the coffee maker and headed right to it. Three cupboards later he found the mugs and poured a full cup. No cream, no sugar. Just black. Pure coffee. Maybe even came from the same mountains they'd driven through. Anticipation built. He took a sip and spat the drink in the sink. Looking around, he saw the familiar blue tin of Maxwell House, then dropped the mug in the sink where it shattered.

"What the hell?" Goya took two steps toward him, hands balling into fists.

"Don't worry," Jack said. "I got another one right here." He grabbed a half-full mug and slammed it against Goya's temple sending him stumbling into the island in the middle of the room.

CHAPTER TWENTY-THREE

Nicolás's kitchen was all steel and marble so it would be a breeze for his workers to clean up once Jack was done dealing with Goya and his men. The island in the center acted as a barricade and prevented the six of them from rushing him all at once. This gave him the upper hand.

Goya crashed to the floor with one hand to his head in an attempt to stem the flood of blood pouring down his face. It seeped through his clenched fingers and across his hand. There was a moment's pause before his men realized what had happened then chaos broke loose. In that split second Jack grabbed a black-handled chef's knife out of the block and brandished it at the man closest to him. The kitchen erupted as seemingly everyone's training kicked in at the same moment.

The man closest to Jack was short and muscular with thick black hair that stood three inches high. Must've taken a tub of grease to get it to stand like that. One slice of the knife across his chest was enough to shock him backward. This gave Jack room to swing upward and drive the knife into the soft flesh under his jaw and up into his brain. He used so much force he could've driven it through the guy's skull but all that hair would have made it impossible to tell. When he pulled the knife free, the man collapsed to the ground in a lifeless lump.

Jack whipped around just in time for a second man, tall and lean, to shove the butt of his shotgun into Jack's stomach. He doubled over and lost his grip on the knife. It clattered to the ground and skated close to Goya's feet.

The lean man brought his knee up. Jack stopped the blow with his crossed forearms then gripped the man's other leg and pulled up on it sweeping him off his feet. The guy landed hard on his side. Jack threw two quick jabs to the man's nose. He heard it crunch after the second blow. He pulled back one more time and slammed his fist into the side of the guy's jaw, knocking him out so he could deal with the three remaining men who had organized themselves as a team.

A young man with a buzz cut raised his weapon to fire on Jack, but the older man next to him pushed the firearm toward the floor. "Not in here, you idiot. Ricochet."

Jack used the distraction to look around the kitchen for another weapon. The workers had left in a hurry and the food they were preparing was still on the stove. Vegetables cooking in grease in a cast iron pan were beginning to burn while potatoes in a large steel pot were boiling over. He grabbed the cast iron pan, ignoring the searing pain of gripping the handle bare handed. He whipped the pan through the air, spraying scorching hot grease and veggies on the man closest to him. Then he brought it back across as he stepped forward. The back side caught the guy on the side of his head, dislocating the guy's jaw and snapping his head halfway around. Once more Jack struck with the cast iron, this time crushing the guy's forehead inward.

He swung around and used it against the man with the broken nose, who had started to get to his feet. One well-placed swing knocked him back into the corner of the counter. He slid to the ground, chin to his chest, blood dripping, body unmoving.

Jack dropped the pan. It felt as though half the skin on his palm went with it. He'd pay for that later. Right now the adrenaline took care of the pain.

The young kid gaped at Jack, but the older man didn't waste time looking at the fate of his comrades. He grabbed a knife and sent the block flying onto the floor behind them so Jack couldn't get to it.

Jack couldn't risk moving backward and tripping over the bodies behind him, so he grabbed a towel hanging from the front of the oven and rushed the older man in front of him. The guy slashed with the knife but was too slow. Jack brought the towel up and wrapped it around the blade and twisted. The guy's hand could only bend so far before he let go of his weapon.

Jack threw a fist into the man's face, driving his arm through and slamming his elbow into the side of the guy's head. The man stumbled and spun in a half circle. Jack stepped forward, wrapped the towel around the guy's throat, turned his back so he held the ends of the towel in front of his chest. He pulled down on the ends until the man was off his feet. Then he lurched forward, yanking out and down, felt the old guy go limp as his neck snapped.

The only one left was the kid. Bear had told Jack about the young one in the woods he'd had no choice but to kill. It wasn't their fault they thought this was the only life they could lead. Hell, Jack understood the call of a good paycheck, even if the work was less than ideal. But everyone had to live with the consequences of their actions. The kid was at least eighteen, so he knew what he was getting into when he charged at Jack.

Taking him was as easy as sliding to the side and using the momentum of the charge to flip him onto the island. Then he drove his fist into the guy's mid-section. As the guy tried to catch his breath, Jack gripped the other man's head in his hands and twisted as hard as he could. There was another crack and the body went still.

Jack surveyed the damage in between heavy inhalations. There were more men inside the place, but he'd dealt with the largest contingent. The rest were patrolling solo or in pairs. It would be easy for Sadie and him to take them out.

Jack wandered back over to the coffee machine and checked the cabinets above for a decent blend. The adrenaline rush was more intense than caffeine, but it didn't last as long. Unfortunately Maxwell House was the only option.

Jack expected to see the glint of the knife near Goya's feet, so when he rounded the corner of the island and it wasn't there, his instincts took over. He stepped back and readied himself a moment before Goya popped up, blade in hand, swinging wildly. The tip of the blade sliced across Jack's ribs, but the wound wasn't deep. Ignoring the sting of the wound, Jack stepped in close so Goya couldn't use the weapon effectively. He threw two jabs. One connected with the soft fleshy area at the base of the neck, and the other his sternum. It had been meant for the man's solar plexus. Instead of doubling over, Goya pushed back, sending Jack into the stove. The edge of the grates seared his lower back. He put his hand back to stop his momentum, further damaging his palm on the burner.

"You think you're getting out of here alive?" Goya stalked toward Jack, forcing him to step over the bodies on the floor. He had the only exit blocked. They both slipped in the blood. Neither was balanced enough to charge the other.

"I've got a better chance than you do, asshole," Jack said.

Goya missed Jack with a wad of spit. "Says who?"

Jack waited until Goya hit a particularly thick patch of blood, his right foot sliding off to the side, before he ducked down behind the island and out of the other man's sight. He snatched one of the knives out of the fallen block and turned the corner of the island, staying low. By the time Goya took two steps forward, Jack popped up behind him on the other side of the island. He whistled to get the other man's attention. When Goya spun around, Jack threw the knife. He clutched his injured hand to his chest after the knife left his grip and watched as the blade sunk dead center in Goya's chest.

"Says the last guy left standing."

Goya collapsed to the ground and Jack nearly collapsed on the island. He needed rest. There'd be time for that later. For now he needed to check in on how Sadie was handling Nicolás.

He grabbed a white towel and wiped his face, neck, arms and hands, turning the linen dark red. The shotgun one of the guys had used to strike him was laying in a puddle of blood. Jack scooped it up and racked it. It wasn't loaded and there weren't any rounds in sight. Why the hell was the guy carrying an unloaded weapon? He pulled the knife from Goya's body, cleaned it on the bloody towel, then left the kitchen and crossed the foyer. He heard low voices coming from the room where Sadie was presumably still meeting with Nicolás. He could bust in there and use the element of surprise against Nicolás, but he knew the other man had a pistol, and Jack only had a knife and an unloaded shotgun. There'd be enough time to kill him in that split second it would take for Nicolás to reach for his weapon, but they needed the man alive if they wanted to find Camila.

So Jack cracked open the door as quietly as he could and peered into the room. As soon as he took in the scene, he pushed the door open wider. He couldn't hold back the surprised chuckle that escaped his mouth.

"How's it going in here?" he asked.

"Pretty good." Sadie didn't look over at him. Nicolás was on his knees in front of her, bloody and beaten. She appeared calm, clean, and a little cocky as she held his own gun to his head. "How about for you?"

Jack looked down at his ripped shirt, his burnt hands, and his bloody jeans. "The coffee here is shit."

CHAPTER TWENTY-FOUR

Franklin was dead. The idiot had gotten cocky. He believed he could take on two of Nicolás's men at once. He'd been knocked down and took two bullets to the brain. We'd hoped to complete the mission without any shots being fired, but shit usually hit the fan in situations like this.

On the plus side it was one less guy I had to take out.

We had discussed the possibility of Goddard sending his men along with us while we took on Nicolás. It was a risk to fight both sides at once but there was the chance some of the senator's team would fall in the meantime.

Unfortunately for me, Spero, Reynard, and McGinnis were actually good at their jobs. We'd fanned out, each man on his own, and surrounded the house. I took out the two men posted out front without much trouble. Franklin had the west side, while Reynard had the east. Spero and McGinnis had circled around to the back and dealt with the teams there.

As soon as my two guys hit the ground I sprinted west in search of Franklin. He was the youngest and the weakest. It wouldn't raise any eyebrows if he'd fallen first. When I turned the corner I saw one of Nicolás's men pull the trigger. The suppressed shot rang out like a pebble hitting a windshield. Discernible for maybe twenty feet or so. I pulled a knife from my hip and threw it with a grunt. It penetrated the guy's throat. Good shot considering I'd tossed on the run. He gurgled and grasped at his neck, but he had no chance. By the time his partner turned around to see what was wrong, I was already standing there. It would have been easier to double-tap with a pistol to the back of his skull.

Wasn't that kind of day.

His eyes grew wide as he looked up at me. I was at least two heads taller and twice as wide. He fumbled his Sig Sauer toward me. I smacked it out of his hand before he had a chance to thread his shaky finger through the trigger guard. Then I bulldozed him over, wrapped my hands around his neck digging my thumbs into his larynx. His face turned red and then dark blue. He tried to break my grip, but his arms were like twigs compared to mine. He brought a knee up aimed for my groin but the shot was weak. I forced him to his knees and then down on his back. I held on until he stopped twitching.

I stopped to pull my knife from the fallen guard's neck, wiping his blood on his shirt. I checked his pockets for a wallet or phone but found nothing useful. Same with his partner. Maybe they were under close surveillance here. All reports had to be made in person to avoid their conversations being picked up.

I had to make a choice. I could cross the front of the house again and try to take down Reynard before he turned the corner to the back of the house. I'd risk being exposed for sure if I did this. The other option was to keep going around the west side and meet the others at the back of the house. The plan from there was to enter in through the rear and assist Jack in finishing off the rest of Nicolás's men.

But Goddard's guys didn't know Sadie was more than just a talented accountant. Her job was to put Nicolás at ease before disarming him. The moment Spero or one of the others saw her with our target, they'd know something was up.

I had to take as many of them out as possible before then.

Decision made, I ran across the front of the house again, a wary eye on the front door. I trusted Jack with my life and knew he could neutralize an entire team of Nicolás's men. But anything could go wrong here. There was a difference between trusting someone and being negligent.

I made it to the east side of the house and ducked low, peering around the corner. Two men lay on the ground. Pools of blood joined together and formed a crimson lake. Reynard leaned over them, breathing heavily, a gash across his arm. He spat on the corpses and looked up in my direction, making sure no one else was on their way to attack him. I pulled back behind the wall just in time.

After a count of ten, I leaned back around the corner and watched Reynard take off for the rear of the house. Gripping an invisible wound on my side, I leaned forward and dragged myself around the corner. A low whistle was all it took to get his attention. He saw my hunched figure slide down the wall and slump forward and he came running. Regardless of how he felt about me, I was still a member of the team, and one less man meant their chances of completing this mission diminished.

I hid my knife in my hand with the blade pressed against my forearm and waited for Reynard to get within an arm's length away. He slowed down when he was near, taking one agonizingly slow step at a time as he scanned the area with a suppressed pistol. Was it for enemies, or me? I let out a groan and slumped forward a little more. I was exposed. He knelt by my side.

"You out, man?" He tucked the pistol behind his back. "What happened?"

I didn't bother answering him. I spun the blade in my hand and stuck the knife deep into the inside of his thigh, reaching up to cover his mouth and silence the scream he couldn't help but unleash. He shoved back at me, swinging to inflict damage to the wound he thought I had. When the blow landed on undamaged skin, his eyes narrowed, finally catching sight of my plan. I didn't give him another moment of contemplation before I shoved the knife through his eye socket, pushing it in to the hilt.

Spero and McGinnis were to wait until the rest of us circled around the back before they entered the house. When none of us showed up, they might separate and check out the east and west sides of the house. One would spot Franklin's dead body and not think anything of it. The young man's long- and short-term chances of survival were slim. It was just a tragedy it had happened so soon, I guess.

The other man would circle around to check on Reynard and notice the two dead bodies and no fellow soldier standing over them. I took Reynard's sidearm then gripped him by the front of his black vest and hooked an arm around his blood-soaked leg. He wasn't a big guy, but damn he was dense. I grunted as I dumped him in the bushes at the front of the house. It wouldn't hide him for long, but when Spero or McGinnis were left by themselves, they'd enter the back of the house on their own. Time wasn't on our side.

That was the thought that propelled me up the front steps and had me stopping at the door. It was a risk going through this way knowing that Nicolás had probably taken Sadie into the same room they had spoken in before. Jack was meant to get the guards away from the two of them and systematically eliminate them, but there was no guarantee it had worked out the way we'd planned.

I saw a shadow pass on the other side of the door and squatted out of sight. A moment passed and no one followed. Was it Jack or one of Nicolás's men? I gripped the doorknob and twisted. It was silent in my hand. Staying low I pushed at the door and stood to the side as it swung open on well-oiled hinges. When I pivoted around the jam, Reynard's suppressed pistol at the ready, I was met with an intriguing scene.

Sadie stood above Nicolás, a gun aimed at his head. He was bleeding from his nose and mouth and there might even have been tears in his eyes. Sadie's face was expressionless. Jack looked as though he'd done battle with a Spartan unit. I stepped inside and closed the door then leaned back against it and smiled. "Rough day at the office?"

Jack shrugged. "I killed a guy with some peppers."

I chuckled. "That's a new one."

Sadie's smile faded. "Why'd you come in through the front?"

I parted the blinds and scoped the entrance. "Change of plans. Franklin and Reynard are down. Spero and McGinnis are gonna come through the back soon."

Jack peered down the hall and then looked up the staircase to the second floor where sunlight spilled in through large skylights. "Rest of the house is empty. With the noise I made in the kitchen, they would've come running if there were any other guards in here. Couple of workers will likely stay out of the way until the coast is clear."

"Tag team?"

Jack nodded. I didn't need to tell him my plan. It was as clear to both of us as the sky outside. He took off up the stairs to double check that the second level was clear and then tucked himself away for the ambush.

I started to pull the door shut on Sadie. "Hang tight, okay?"

"Be careful."

I took off down the hall and met Spero and McGinnis as soon as they breached the rear entrance.

"Where the hell is everyone?" Spero looked me up and down. "Where'd you come from? Whose blood is that?"

"Front door." I took a couple deep, sharp breaths like I'd been put through the ringer. "You hear those shots? Franklin's down. Pulled one of the men in here out through the front door. I didn't have a choice."

"Seen Reynard?" McGinnis asked.

I looked around like I just noticed he wasn't standing there with us. "Where is he?"

"Hell if I know." Spero gestured with his head in the direction behind me. "What's going on out there?"

"Jack took out the guys down here. He's got Nicolás, but he didn't have a chance to clear the second floor. Let's go."

I knew Spero didn't like taking directions from me, but I was already on the move. The threat of the unknown upstairs was bigger than his problems with me. And with me leading the way I had them at my back. It would put them at ease, even though it was a false sense of security. They had no idea what was waiting for them.

The three of us crept up the stairs as silently as the wooden steps would allow. As soon as I hit the landing, I took off to the right. Spero took off left, directing McGinnis to follow me. I stopped at the first door and looked back at him. He nodded his head and twisted the knob and pushed it open slowly. When no one jumped out, I stepped inside, quickly taking in the spacious bedroom. It held a wide cherry bed and a matching desk and dresser. I crossed to the left side of the room. McGinnis took the right to clear the bathroom.

I made it look like I was going to check the closet, but as soon as he stepped out of view I circled around and slipped into the confined room. His eyes caught mine in the mirror. I had to act a second sooner than I planned. Instead of a perfect kill strike, I swung my knife down into his shoulder, then kicked his legs out from underneath him. His head smacked the porcelain sink. As he went down I wrapped my hand around his jaw to both pull him up and to keep him from calling out. I pulled his head back against my torso and slid the knife across his throat and ended him right then and there.

I left the body on the floor and crossed back around the room. As soon as I entered the hallway, I heard a crash from the direction Spero had walked in. I charged into a room at the far end of the hallway where Jack and Spero grappled hand-to-hand. Noble had years of martial arts experience but it looked as though Spero might give him a run for his money.

Jack looked up when I entered the room. He gave me a slight nod, then managed to get enough leverage to push Spero several steps back. The other man still had no idea I was there. I crept forward and dug my knife into his spleen. He cried out, twisting away. Jack landed three heavy blows to his gut, and then drove Spero's head down into his knee.

Spero fell off to the side. His nose was bent an inch or two to the left. Blood poured over his mouth. Jack looked down at him. "Guess you were right about us all along."

"Fuck you." Spero choked on his blood.

"Maybe next time." Jack looked up at me.

I pulled out Reynard's suppressed Beretta, racked the slide and chambered a round, and fired three rounds into Spero's head. "Phase one complete."

"Now for the hard part."

CHAPTER TWENTY-FIVE

The safe house was ten miles from Nicolas's place. The final stretch was a dirt road littered with potholes. The sedan bounced and pitched and swayed. The AC stopped working along the way. Dirt and dust rode in on the wind and settled on the dash, the seats, and us. The air felt moist. A glance to the west revealed dark clouds headed in from the Pacific. I had a feeling a hell of a storm was brewing.

The banging from the trunk didn't phase us. Nicolás had been gagged before we threw him in. His ankles were tied together, so were his wrists. A foot-long length of rope connected the two.

The three-story home stood out against the dark clouds a quarter-mile away. Not necessarily a bad thing. Not great either. Sadie slowed to a crawl as she navigated the long driveway. I made no move to hide the AR-15 I'd taken from Nicolás's place on the way out. Thirty rounds gave me plenty of leeway. Sadie pulled up to the side of the house and shifted into park.

Jack and I cleared the house, floor by floor, room by room. Sadie remained outside. If anyone turned toward the house she'd fire her pistol to warn us and then drive off with our prisoner.

It didn't come to that.

We carried Nicolás inside to the second floor. Jack and I and pinned him down in a chair while Sadie tied his legs to the base and then secured his torso. Even if he managed to free himself, he wouldn't get far. The three of us would take him down within seconds.

Nicolás had one eye swollen shut and a large gash above the other. Blood still trickled from his nose and corner of his mouth. Sadie was not to be messed with, it seemed. I stared down at him, showing no emotion. He met my stare. His arms strained against the rope and he extended both middle fingers and aimed them at me.

"That ain't gonna get you nowhere," I said. "Except maybe down to eight fingers when you leave here."

The man leaned his head back and then spat a bloody wad of saliva at Sadie. She moved her head in time but couldn't get completely out of the way. The mess hit her sleeve.

"You son of a bitch." She reared back and drove her open palm into his groin. His face twisted as an empty howl passed his lips. She rose and took a couple steps back. Her hand rested on the Glock 19 she had tucked into her waistband.

He stared up at her with a pained expression that went deeper than his crushed gonads. "You bitch. You think you can deceive me like this? Who are these men?"

"You haven't told him yet?" I asked.

"I figured you guys would want to watch this."

The guy had complicated her job in more ways than one. It was time for her revenge.

"You figured right," Jack said.

Sadie looked at me, then at Jack, then back down at Nicolás. It was impossible to gauge her feelings by looking at her face. "I'm not who you think I am. I'm not an accountant. I'm not Michelle. I am in no way involved with your pathetic ass. I work for the CIA, Nicolás, and I've been playing you from day one."

Nicolás stared down at his hands, eyes wide. Then his nostrils flared, his lips drew tight, his eyes narrowed. He fought against his ropes, tipping his chair over. Jack caught it and righted the man. "I'm going to destroy you." He looked wildly around the room, then shouted, "All of you."

Sadie pulled the sidearm from her hip and pressed the barrel against his groin, making him go still. "You're not in a position to talk to me like that, Nicolás." She was cold and calculating. Hardly the woman he'd come to know over the years.

"What are you saying?" He shook his head, smiled. "The CIA has been watching me this whole time?"

Sadie's lips twitched. "Are you serious? You think you're worth anything more than a passing glance? Your uncle was the mission. Then eventually Goddard. You were barely on our board."

Nicolás's face went another shade darker. "When I get out of this—"

Jack leaned down. "When you get out of this, if you get out of this, you're going to prison. Which is a best-case scenario, buddy. Your man Goddard is getting a personalized bullet. Count your blessings."

I stepped forward. "We know you have the girl." Nicolás's head snapped in my direction. "Where is she?"

His lips parted as a wide grin spread over his face. Sadie had knocked out at least three of his teeth and broken two others. If he kept that smile on his face, he might lose a few more. His eyebrows rose and he stared at her. "I guess you don't hold all the cards after all, do you?" He started laughing.

My hand shot out and I punched him in the face. His head snapped back then rebounded forward. Nicolás spit fresh blood onto the floor an inch from Jack's shoe. Jack pinned the man down with a look.

"You don't want to test me today, man."

"And you don't want to push my buttons," Nicolás said. "I know where the girl is. You won't get her until you let me go." He looked at each of us in turn, perhaps trying to isolate the weakest of us. "Seems like a fair trade."

"Except for the part where you walk free. Not gonna happen."

Sadie stepped forward, holding her arms out to keep both me and Jack at bay. She looked down at the man in the chair. "Look, we're going to find her eventually. You help us now and I'll protect you. I'll tell my bosses you were cooperative."

"And if I don't?"

I took a gamble. "Then we turn you over to Goddard like we were meant to from the beginning. You think jail is worse than what that asshole and his deranged security guys will do to you? Who knows where you'll end up if you're in his hands. He's got more power down here than the CIA. You might not even get to a torture cell. You'll only get a grave if you're lucky. He may just want to make an example out of you."

Nicolás stared at his hands. I could see him weighing his options.

Jack pulled out his cell. "You've got ten seconds. I'm calling Goddard. You get to decide what I tell him."

He licked the blood off his lips, swallowed hard. "What happens if I play your game?"

Sadie gestured toward us. "Then we keep you safe until we take Goddard out ourselves. Either way, you're at the end of your rope. You better make the right decision."

"Five seconds," Jack said.

Nicolás struggled against his bindings again. He grunted, then went slack with a raspy sigh.

Jack hit the call button and held the phone up to his ear. "What's it gonna be?"

Nicolás's face scrunched up. He spoke through his clenched jaw. "I'll tell you where she is. But you better hold up your end of the bargain. If anyone shows up there without me, she's dead."

The attention of the room switched over to Jack as soon as Goddard answered the phone. He put the call on speaker. "It's done. Nicolás is dead."

"Good." There was a rustle of paper in the background and the sound of a drawer sliding shut. "And his men?"

"Taken out. It was a bloody fight and there were losses on our side, too. But we shouldn't have any trouble from here on out."

"So I suppose you really are as good as Michelle said. Is she safe?"

Jack looked up at Sadie, who stepped closer to the phone. She let a waver of emotion enter her voice. "I'm here. Everything's okay. They kept me safe."

"Good. Good." There was a pause. "Put Spero on the phone."

Jack met my gaze. "He already took off. Franklin went down and Reynard took a knife to the side. Once we cleared the house, Spero split."

Goddard hesitated a moment before he answered. It sounded like he drummed his fingers near the phone's speaker. "That doesn't sound like him."

"Hell if I know." Jack spoke quick and gruff. "I got Bear and Michelle with me. You want us to go after him?"

Another pause. "No. Head back. Bring me Nicolás's body."

"Can't we just take a picture, man? Not too keen on hauling a body around in a car. Things would get messy real quick if we got pulled over."

"Then don't get pulled over. Bring me Nicolás's body. Don't make me tell you a third time." The line went silent.

Jack slipped the phone in his back pocket, then turned to Nicolás. "We did what we said we'd do. Your turn."

"So I can tell you where she is and you can bring my body to Goddard after all? No way, man."

Sadie opened her mouth to argue when a ringtone went off. It took a moment to pinpoint the sound. Jack stepped forward and pulled a phone from Nicolás's pocket. The name Vasquez lit up the screen.

Jack turned the phone toward Nicolás. "You expecting a call?"

Nicolás's eyebrows drew together separated by a fine line that traversed his forehead. "I don't know why he's calling me. We don't have any business with one another. It all goes through Goddard."

"Any idea what it could be about?" Jack said.

Nicolás thought for a moment. "Could be a heads up for Goddard. Rumor has it Vasquez holds a grudge."

"A grudge for what?" I asked.

"Hell if I know."

The phone stopped ringing. We all stared at it for a couple heartbeats, then it lit up again.

"Better answer it," I said. "Only way to find out."

Jack tapped the speaker button. He waited for Vasquez to say something first.

The other man's voice filled the room. "Hello, Mr. Noble."

My head snapped up. How could he possibly know Jack was with Nicolás, much less that he answered the phone? Sadie crossed the room and looked out through the window. After a moment, she turned back to us and shook her head. There was no one out there.

"And Riley is there too, I presume?" Vasquez said. "And Michelle? Though I doubt that's her real name. I still haven't tracked down her real identity, but it's only a matter of time. Don't be shy. Speak up."

"What the hell do you want?" Jack said.

"Ah, Jack, you need to work on your bedside manner." Vasquez laughed. He knew he had taken us by surprise and was basking in it. "All right, all right. Here's what I want."

There was a weight in my stomach that made me feel as though I was going to crash through the floor at any minute.

Vasquez cleared his throat. "Kill Thomas Goddard within the next twelve hours or I'll tell him exactly who you all are."

CHAPTER TWENTY-SIX

J ack tossed Nicolás's phone on the floor and strode over to the window. He threw it open with a couple of strong heaves. A warm gust blew in, disturbing some papers on a corner table. The room smelled like gardenias. He wiped the sweat from his brow, shook it off, then grabbed Nicolás by the back of the collar and dragged him to the wall. The chair screeched on the red tile floor like fingernails down a chalkboard. I gritted against the sound. He cut the ropes binding the man to the chair and hoisted him headfirst through the window. Sadie and I lurched forward. Jack threw up one hand to keep us at bay. He had the man secured at the ankles. The soles of his shoes were all I saw.

All bluster was gone. Nicolás was screaming his head off.

"I'm going to say this one time, asshole. We're going to save that girl, then we're going to kill Goddard, and then I'm going to deal with Vasquez personally. The only unknown factor here is whether you live or die, and that depends on what you choose to tell me right now."

Nicolás was trying to flail his limbs to keep his balance, but his wrists and ankles were still bound. His screams intensified. We didn't care. There were no houses for miles in either direction. He could make all the noise he wanted.

Jack let the guy even further out the window. I resisted the urge to pull him back. I had no love for the guy, but a girl's life was on the line. Jack was taking a big gamble.

"My grip is slipping. Keep screaming. No one is going to hear you out here. Not even when you hit the ground."

"All right, all right!" Nicolás yelled. "All right! I'll tell you."

"Tell me now before I accidentally let you go." Jack was starting to strain against the man's thrashing. It was taking all his strength to keep him from diving head first into the concrete.

"She's at my uncle's safehouse. It's a cottage outside the city. I can take you there."

Jack started to pull the guy up, then hesitated and let him slide back out a couple inches at a time. Was he thinking about letting him go?

"Jack." Sadie said, perhaps sharing my concern. "If he takes us there, we can keep an eye on him. If he's lying, we can deal with that then."

"I'm not lying."

"Jack."

Jack glanced back at Sadie. His wild eyes calmed and he nodded. He turned back to the window and stuck his head out to look at Nicolás. "Make no mistake about it. If you're lying to me, I will kill you slowly and painfully. You'll beg me to bring you back here and drop you out of this window."

Jack pulled Nicolás inside and let him crash to the tile floor head first. His scalp split open under his hairline. Somehow the guy had the wherewithal to keep his mouth shut. Jack looked around the room before snatching Nicolás's phone off the ground and heading down the stairs.

Sadie glanced over at me, mouth open. "The hell was that?"

I pushed a breath of air through pursed lips. "It has been a long day."

BLOOD MIXED WITH SWEAT AND SETTLED INTO NICOLÁS'S eyebrow. Sadie found a dirty rag and tied it around the guy's head to stop the blood flow. We secured his hands behind him. He seemed to have achieved some state of zen and remained calm while seated on the floor. A lot of men were all bluster until they met someone with less respect for life than themselves. A solid brush with death will put anyone's existence in perspective.

"Jack's already outside," Sadie said. "You ready?" She glanced down at our prisoner.

I reached down and picked the guy up. He went limp, his spoiled ass resigned to the fact that he had no choice in the matter. His blood trickled down my triceps and around my elbow. It settled into the hair on my forearm. Halfway down the stairs I knocked his head into the wall. The guy didn't make a sound. Sadie opened the front door, peeked outside, then stepped out of the way so I could clear the entryway without further damaging Nicolás.

Jack was leaning up against the car, arms crossed, eyes closed, facing the sun. He looked like a wolf soaking it in after a long cold winter. Behind his closed eyelids he sensed everything around him. Saw it outlined in the heat signatures the bright light offered. His cheeks and forehead were red. His hair rose and fell with the wind.

"Everyone cool as cats now, huh?" I said.

The trance was broken. He opened his eyes, shrugged and circled around to the other side of the car. "You got him, big man?"

"Yeah." I pulled Nicolás off my shoulder and opened the rear door. A cloud of dust rose off the seat. I tossed the guy into the back and forced him to move over so I wouldn't have to walk around. He did so without any grumbling. Sadie slid in behind the wheel and Jack jumped into the passenger seat.

Sadie's lips were pursed. "Where to, Nicolás?"

"Start driving." He jutted his chin straight ahead. "It'll take an hour or so."

Jack twisted around in his seat. Nicolás shrunk back. "We going to have any trouble?"

"Can I count on you to talk to someone and tell them I did what you asked? Grant me immunity?"

"As long as you fall in line, I can make a couple of calls."

He'd never do it. Immunity meant a free pass to a guy like Nicolás. He'd go straight for a week, maybe a month. Hell, the guy might last a year without committing a felony. But sooner or later the draw of the life would be stronger than working for minimum wage at the Gas N' Go. Before long, he'd start to rebuild the empire he never fully had a grasp on. He'd come so close to achieving his dream. Give him a second chance and he'd go right back to work on it.

Nicolás leaned his head back and closed his eyes. "Then we won't have any trouble."

Jack twisted back around in his seat. "Good man."

Sadie put the car in drive and launched us forward. The tires skated along the loose dirt before gaining traction. Plumes of dust rose in our wake.

Jack decided against calling Javier. There was no point in getting the man's hopes up. Besides, he'd want to know where we were heading. If he showed up emotion would rule the game. Nothing good would come from that. It was better to deliver no news than to create bad news. And even better to stay quiet and surprise someone with exactly the news they were hoping to hear.

The drone of the engine and the road filled the car. Nicolás only spoke when he instructed Sadie to make a turn here or there. His voice was low, calm, and empty. He was defeated in every sense of the word. I caught Sadie glancing at him in the rearview every couple of miles. She seemed more confused than concerned. She'd known him for years, had seen the extent of his cruelty. Maybe she'd even felt it once or twice. Now he was a broken man in comparison. But that's what happens when all hope is lost. You give in. You die. Even if your body still lives. Nicolás had it all for a few fleeting moments.

Now he'd learned that being at the top only means you have further to fall.

And they all fall.

I watched the countryside turn into the outline of the city and fade back again, occasionally turning toward Nicolás to make sure he wasn't trying anything. He was almost pathetic to watch and after about half an hour I stopped checking on him as often. He wasn't part of the equation anymore, which worked out in our favor, except now Vasquez had replaced him. That didn't bode well.

I leaned forward between the seats, surprising Sadie and making her jump. The car swerved just a little bit and she scowled at me over her shoulder. People always underestimate how well I move for a guy who's six-six.

Since the phone call, something had been bothering me. Vasquez had too much information. I tapped Jack on the shoulder. "How does he know who you are?"

Jack rubbed his temple for a few seconds. "I don't know, man. Been wondering that as well. He's working with different information than Goddard."

"And why does he want Goddard dead?" I turned back to Nicolás to see if he had any other information to share.

"I don't know. The two of them have been working together for a while. I didn't know anything was off between them until recently." Nicolás turned to the window. The wind rush blew his hair off the bloody rag covering the wound on his forehead. "Make a right up here. We're almost there."

I leaned back in my seat and continued watching the scenery go by. The suburbs gave way to trees and fields, and soon Nicolás instructed Sadie to turn and five minutes later pull off to the side of the road.

"The cottage is about a mile up ahead," he said.

"Anyone patrolling the property or surrounding woods?" Jack asked.

Nicolás shook his head. "There's four guys inside. Two out front, one at the rear, and the last keeping an eye on the girl."

"You're a piece of shit, you know that, right?"

Nicolás looked away, shook his head, as though he wanted to say more. Maybe he was going to apologize. Maybe he had an excuse. No one particularly cared what it was either way, and it seemed like he knew that. He snapped his mouth shut and turned back to the window.

Sadie pulled out her gun. "You two go on ahead. I'll keep an eye on him."

Jack opened his door, placed one foot on the ground, looked back at Sadie. "Anyone else comes from that direction other than us and a little girl, you shoot first and ask questions later. Dump him in a ditch and get the hell out of there."

She racked her Glock's slide. "Copy that."

Jack and I waited for a large truck to pass, then dashed into the woods. We led with our pistols. We were far enough out in the country that a couple of shots wouldn't cause unwanted attention, and even if it did, we would be out of there before the authorities arrived.

I led the way through the trees, as quickly and quietly as I could. This was my domain. I'd grown up in the backwoods of North Carolina. Give me a forest anywhere in the world and I was home. I sucked in a deep breath and inhaled the mix of dirt, bugs, life, decay. Dead leaves and twigs crunched underfoot. For now that was acceptable. Once we were closer to the house more precautions would have to be taken.

It had been a couple of days since Camila had been taken. Nicolás was hardly a humanitarian, but I doubted he was a big enough asshole to keep her locked up without food and water. Then again he was a big enough asshole to kidnap a ten-year-old in the first place. Anything was possible at this point.

The woods opened into a small clearing. A tiny one-room wooden cottage sat dead center. As soon as we walked up to the last tree, I stopped and looked back at Jack. We were close to rescuing the girl. This sideways adventure in Costa Rica was about to come to an end. I lifted my eyebrows and nodded at him.

He peered around me before meeting my eyes. Something was wrong.

CHAPTER TWENTY-SEVEN

The door swung on one hinge with the wind gusts. A pair of bodies lay slumped against the jam. Even from a distance I could see the holes in their foreheads, the dried blood on their faces and clothes. Jack climbed the steps first and stole a glance inside. Soft music escaped through the opening. He turned to me and shook his head.

I gestured toward the side of the house. Jack nodded and turned back to the front door. We'd been working together so long little had to be said or done to communicate our intentions. Chances anyone was left alive inside were slim. Jack could handle it on his own even if someone was lying in wait. I just hoped the only dead we came across were anyone but Camila.

I turned the corner of the cottage and crept along the side, scanning the wood's edge. When I reached the end, I eased around the corner. I kept my pistol a couple feet ahead of my sight line. There was one more body lying on the ground. Feeling certain he was just as dead as the first two, I moved forward and kicked him over. He had bullet wounds to the chest, abdomen, and a single shot in the center of his forehead.

The back door was simple and wooden. It hadn't been kicked off its hinges like the front, so I grasped the knob and twisted it slowly. When I felt it unlatch, I threw it open and stepped inside. Jack peered back at me, his pistol raised.

The cottage was very nearly a single room as Nicolás had described. The minimalist kitchen opened to the living room, which housed a sofa and a pair of chairs. The fabric was worn and faded and patched up in a couple spots. A small TV sat on one leaning wooden cart, hooked up with a couple of gaming systems. A body lay slumped across the couch. We didn't bother checking his pulse. Half his head had been blown away.

"Three guesses who got here before we did," Jack said.

"I'm glad we decided not to tell Javier about this place. He'd have a breakdown on the spot."

Jack shook his head and cursed at the walls. "Vasquez is playing a goddamn game with us."

Jack pulled a buzzing phone from his pocket . He looked up at me and ground his teeth, then answered and hit the speaker.

"Hello, Mr. Noble."

"Vasquez."

"I assume you've made it to the cottage by now. Nicolás should've known better than to keep her there. Amateur move on his part, which is what I would expect from him."

"Where's the girl?"

"With me. Safe. I won't harm a hair on her head unless you decide to keep ignoring my directives. You have a little more than ten hours now to complete the task. Kill Goddard and you will get sweet Camila back."

"She's just a kid."

"I know, Jack. I know. I have children, too. They're all grown up now, but my grandkids are the light of my life. They keep me good. They keep me grounded. Goddard threatened them. Did you know that?"

Jack said nothing.

"He did. And though he has not acted on his threats, I fear it is time for me to eliminate the chance that he will. I want him dead."

"All you had to do was ask," Jack said. "Guess that was too hard for you. But this? You're willing to kill an innocent girl to ensure this happens?"

"Yes." Vasquez's voice went hard. "My family before anyone else's. I don't want to hurt her, Jack, but I will. Goddard's own family is unfortunately out of reach, otherwise I would let sweet Camila go and take them instead. Unless something changes, she will have to be my insurance that Goddard is killed."

"And why don't you do it yourself? Set up a meeting and take care of him there. You don't even have to use a weapon. Poison takes longer. It's more fun."

Vasquez laughed. "You know better than that. The cleaner my hands on this job, the better. I'm not asking for fame. That's the last thing I want. I just need my revenge, and I'll be happy."

"You're a bastard."

"In point of fact, I am." Vasquez paused. "You have ten hours, Mr. Noble."

IT TOOK US HALF THE AMOUNT OF TIME TO GET BACK TO THE car. There was little regard to how much noise we made. I picked a line and led the way, deviating as necessary. All the sweet smells of the forest were lost on me now. In the thick jungle the wind died early amid the tangle of brush and vines. The humidity was killer, my body drenched with sweat. Pain ate at my muscles and joints with every thud of my feet. Hunger pangs filled my stomach. But we had to push on and get to the car quickly.

Sadie stared from within the dusty Camry. Her side mirror glinted in a brief moment of sunlight. Her pistol was aimed in our direction. Without the girl, she had no reason to believe it was us until we got closer. We kept our hands in view and exited the trees slowly and deliberately. Once we were in sight she lowered her firearm.

Nicolás leaned out the door, which Sadie had opened to presumably give him some air. It would be stifling in that tin can at this point during the day. Still, it wasn't a great idea. If he tried to escape, she'd have to deal with it. That meant time out in the open. The road didn't have much traffic, but we weren't privy to when there'd be a passerby.

"Where is she?" he asked.

"Not there," Jack said.

He shrunk back inside the car. "I swear I was telling the truth. She was there. She was there with four of my men. Two out front, one out back, and—"

"And one inside," I finished. "Yeah, we verified that. They're all dead."

Sadie emerged from the car and grabbed my arm. "Any trace of the girl?""

"Gone." I freed myself from her grip. "Vasquez has her."

"How do you know?"

"He called me." Jack gripped the phone tightly in his hand. He looked as though he wanted to toss it against the side of the car, but thought better of destroying the only line of communication he had with Vasquez. With Javier's daughter.

"What now?" Sadie asked.

I wiped a line of sweat from the top of my lip. "Kill Goddard, hope Vasquez keeps his word."

"We can't take that risk." She stepped back and blocked the opening to the driver's seat.

"We might not have a choice." I drew a line in the dirt with the tip of my shoe. "Vasquez seems smart. Hell, he knows our moves before we make them. He's not going to be as stupid or as easy to crack as this idiot. I don't think we're gonna be able to find her."

Nicolás looked up sharply, as though he was going to say something smart to me. He thought better of it and leaned back inside the car.

Jack reached into the backseat and pulled out his jacket. He reached into the pocket and brought out a pair of sunglasses. He made to place them on his head, but he paused and stared down at the shades with his brows knitted.

"What is it?" I asked.

After a moment's pause Jack turned toward Nicolás. "Who told you about the hit?"

"What?"

Jack grabbed Nicolás out of the back of the car and pushed him up against the Camry. "Who told you about the hit on Goddard?"

"I don't know his name."

"Bullshit." Jack punched Nicolás in the gut.

I moved in position next to him. I leaned in and said, "What is it?"

Jack said nothing. He drove his knee into the man's midsection and let him fall to the ground.

"I seriously don't know." Nicolás coughed to regain his breath. Dirt mixed with his sweat and caked the left half of his face. "I got a call from a guy. He was an American. He told me about a hit going down on Goddard. Said if I wanted things to work out in my favor, I'd make sure it happened on my terms."

Jack knelt and smacked Nicolás across the face. "And you never questioned why this mysterious man was handing you Goddard on a silver platter? Come on. Are you really that stupid?"

"Of course I did. I'm not an idiot." His gaze slid over to me then shot back to Jack. He flinched when Jack rocked back on his heels. "It's not like I got any answers. He just told me who Javier was and where we could find Camila. I've got a couple contacts and I had them and my guys looking into who could've made the call, but we didn't come up with anything. I figured I'd deal with the possible consequences when they came through."

"And that's why you'd never be as good of a leader as your uncle." Sadie crossed her arms and leaned against the car, an eyebrow raised in challenge. Nicolás didn't say anything. "You think he would've let this happen?"

I copied Sadie's posture. "What are you thinking, Jack?"

Jack finally let Nicolás go and started pacing along the length of the car. "Whoever called him gave him Javier's identity, which means he knew who we were, too. But he didn't tell Nicolás about us. Why?"

I furrowed my brow. "Must've had a reason."

"He wanted to screw with the op but he was keeping our identities close to the chest."

"Probably until it worked in his favor to reveal them," Sadie said.

"So what game are they playing?" I said.

Jack shook his head. "I don't know, man, but I got a pretty good idea of who made that phone call." He held out Thorne's sunglasses to me.

I took them. The reflection of my dirty face filled both lenses. "Why would he want to mess with the op?"

Sadie threw out her hands. "Who?"

Jack turned toward her. "A man named Thorne. He works for Skinner. He's the only other person that knew about this." Jack looked back at me over his shoulder. "We were set up from the beginning."

CHAPTER TWENTY-EIGHT

"Thorne?" I couldn't help sounding dismissive of the suggestion. "He's nobody. Why would he want to mess with our op?"

"I don't know that he does." Jack continued pacing. He rubbed the stubble on his chin. "He didn't tell Nicolás who we were. He gave him Javier's identity, as well as Camila's, and he told Nicolás to hold off on having Goddard killed until the time was right."

"So there's a reason why he extended the op, why he wanted Goddard left alive." I started moving in Jack's footsteps. "He was waiting for something."

"What's Goddard working on back home?"

"Hell if I know. Wasn't pertinent to the job. I didn't look into it any further. Did you?"

Jack shook his head. "We need to know."

"We don't have much time. Ten hours and counting."

Sadie stepped forward. "Does it work out in our favor at all if we don't kill Goddard? What if we just go after Vasquez?"

"I don't think that's going to work." Jack put his hands on his hips and leaned his head back. "Javier wouldn't hear of it."

"What he doesn't know doesn't hurt him?" I shrugged.

Jack met my gaze. "The girl is our number one priority. Goddard was our primary mission anyway. If we take him out, we kill two birds with one stone."

"Three," I said, "if it means screwing up Thorne's plans."

"How do you know it's Thorne, though?" Sadie asked. "Couldn't it come from the top?"

"Frank?" Bear said.

Jack laughed. "Absolutely. But Frank handed us the op. I don't see why he'd do that just to take it away from us. No, someone else has is involved. Maybe it's not Thorne, but he's the most likely suspect at this point. I just can't see why."

I wiped the sweat from my brow. "Do we talk to Frank?"

"Frank doesn't pussyfoot around. He'd go right to Thorne, and we can't risk him finding out that we're on to him. The more relaxed he feels about getting away with pulling strings, the easier it's gonna be to catch him at it later."

"Okay then what's the plan?"

Jack looked at each of us in turn. "We go after Goddard and pray Vasquez turns over the girl. We hand her and Nicolás to Javier, make sure Camila is secure, and then we take down Vasquez. Once he's out of the picture, we're on our way home and Thorne's gonna find out why we get paid contract rates for our work."

"Works for me," I said.

Sadie nodded.

When Jack turned to Nicolás, the other man just shrugged. "Better than a death sentence, I guess."

Jack opened the passenger side door. "Let's roll."

THE REST OF THE CAR RIDE WAS SPENT ARGUING OVER WHETHER Sadie would join us on our mission to kill Goddard. She wanted to be there. She wanted to be the one to put a bullet in his brain after all these years. She wanted him to look up at her and realize she had been playing him the whole time. If anyone was gonna obliterate the op she'd worked on for so long, it had to be her.

Jack didn't want to take that from her, but there was the little problem of the man in the back seat.

"You can just leave me in the car," Nicolás said.

The hope in his voice was comical. I couldn't help but laugh. "In another life, I might have liked you, man. You're an idiot, but you're a funny idiot."

Nicolás scowled back at me. There'd been a change in him. He'd been taken down a peg. All that undeserved power he'd garnered from being related to his uncle had gone to his head. It hadn't been a flattering look on him. Not that this broken version was much better. A marginal improvement at best. I no longer wanted to knock out the rest of his teeth every time he opened his mouth.

Sadie kept the gas down to the floor. She wanted to get back to the city as quickly as possible. Now that we had a plan, everyone was looking forward to seeing it through. "Let's call in Javier and catch him up. We can drop Nicolás off, take him off the board. You need me more than we need him with us."

"I have a rapport with Goddard now," Jack said. "We don't need you to get in the door."

He didn't mean to be dismissive, but his words rankled at her.

"Jesus, Jack. I've been undercover for years. I've wasted my life here. You think you deserve to be there more than me?"

"It's not about who deserves to be there or not." He popped open the glove box but didn't take anything out. "It's what makes the most logical sense."

Sadie released one hand from the wheel and dug into her outer leg pocket. Jack was so busy digging through the contents of the glove box that he didn't notice until it was too late. Before he could swat the phone out of her hand, she dialed a number and hit send with more force than necessary and had the phone up to her ear.

"We've got Nicolás." There was a pause. "No, he doesn't know

where she is. We need to drop him off with you. We're heading over
to Goddard's now to figure out the next step. She's close. I know she
is. We'll get her."

Jack's fists were balled up on his lap, but he didn't reach for the
phone. If he had, he might not have kept his hand.

"Be there in forty." Sadie hung up and slammed her phone down
into the cup holder cracking the screen. "See? Problem solved."

"You shouldn't have done that. Javier's desperate. If he thinks
Nicolás doesn't have Camila, he's gonna start making bold moves.
He's got resources, assets, that he can call off of their assignments.
You don't know what kind of ripple effect this could have."

She relaxed her grip on the wheel. "Then we better wrap this up
sooner rather than later."

"You're putting a girl's life in danger."

Sadie slammed on the brakes so suddenly that it launched me
forward into the back of her seat. Nicolás threw up his tied hands and
stopped himself from smacking his face into the back of Jack's head-
rest. Noble cursed. A horn honked behind us. A station wagon with
wood paneled sides passed us by. The driver threw his hands up in
anger but didn't bother stopping to chew us out. Probably best
for him.

"You will not take this from me, Jack." Sadie's voice was deadly
still. "Javier won't do anything that could put Camila in danger. She's
all he cares about. Admit that you just don't want me there because
you have it in your head that you need to keep me safe."

Jack looked like she'd slapped him. "You're an agent for the CIA
who has clearly managed to survive in this ecosystem for several
years. Why the hell would I feel like I need to keep you safe?"

"Because you're a man? Because you don't think I can handle
myself? Because you have a history of losing the people around you,
so you constantly overcompensate by taking those choices away
from them."

"Don't use bullshit psychology on me, Sadie. Keep that to
yourself."

She'd struck a nerve with him. I leaned forward. "We don't have time for this."

Sadie gestured at Jack while accelerating past the station wagon. "Tell him that."

I turned to Jack. "Look, man, I get it. She's one more back we gotta watch. But we could use her. She'll get us in close to Goddard. Having an extra set of hands isn't going to hurt us. She knows what she's signing up for. She deserves to have this. And even if he suspects us, she can strike without notice, without suspicion. It might go down smoother with her there."

Jack blew out a breath and cracked his neck from side to side. I felt the warm wind blow in through the windows and slam into my face for the first time. The next sixty seconds might as well have been an hour. When he answered he was much calmer. "It's not that I don't think you can handle it."

"Then what is it?" Sadie's voice was still sharp.

Jack laughed humorlessly. "If things don't go as planned, if it gets out of hand, Goddard will use you against us. Do you understand who we are?"

She glanced over, said nothing.

"I mean who we really are? If you don't then pull over and get out now, because every inch we take forward cements you further into this, and I will not be held liable for the decisions I have to make to get this job done."

There was a moment of silence in the car. I couldn't help myself. "I'm offended."

Sadie looked at me from the rearview mirror, an eyebrow raised.

"Known this son of a bitch for years. I'm still not good enough to be used for leverage against him. He'd sooner let me die than drop his weapon."

"Nah, man, I'd just shoot right through you. You can't get any uglier as it is."

Even Nicolás chuckled. I shot him a look and he knew well

enough to turn in the other direction, though there was still a smile on his face.

"So you're just trying to keep me pretty?" There was finally some humor in Sadie's voice.

"Exactly." Jack's face turned serious. "Look, forget I said anything. You're right. You deserve to be there. But it's a tossup between who gets to pull the trigger."

"You're on."

I leaned forward again. "Count me in."

Nicolás turned back to us. "What about me?"

"Not a chance."

"Nice try."

"You're going away for a long time, man."

Nicolás shrugged. "It was worth the try."

THE SCENE OUTSIDE THE COMPOUND WAS UNLIKE BEFORE. There were several vehicles parked on the grounds. Javier sent three of his men out to meet us. They took Nicolás by the arm and shoved him into the back of a sedan with heavily tinted windows. The guy shot a look back at us that I had trouble reading. Was he saying goodbye? Had he changed his mind and wanted us to take him back?

Two of the men climbed into the vehicle. The third approached and told us that Javier was busy working another angle to find his daughter and that he'd be in touch with us shortly. We should proceed as planned.

"I almost feel bad for the guy," I said as the sedan pulled away.

Jack shot me a look. "Seriously?"

I shrugged. "In another life he could've been a funny guy."

Sadie started to walk back to the Camry, driving her shoulder into me as she passed. "In this life he was a killer. He doesn't get a chance at another life, even a hypothetical one."

We all slid back into the car. Jack caught her eye. "You feel bad?"

"About turning him in?"

"That." He chose his words carefully. "And the fact that he wasn't the man you hoped he could've been."

Sadie started the car and slowly pulled away from the compound. When she spoke, I heard the conviction in her voice. "No. He had his chance. He proved he wasn't interested in being a better man. I can understand living in gray areas. We all do it. But I won't stand for someone who consistently chooses themselves over others. There's no hope for people like that."

I caught the strain on Jack's face as he looked out the window. We both struggled with being good men, but perhaps Jack more so than most.

CHAPTER TWENTY-NINE

"I s it done?" Goddard stood at the top of the concrete steps, his hand on his stomach as though he'd just finished a healthy meal.

The three of us made it halfway from the Camry to the front door before we were met by his security detail. They approached with weapons drawn. They patted us down and stripped us of our pistols. This would not be an easy fight.

Jack hooked a thumb over his shoulder. "Body's in the trunk. With the heat and humidity we don't want to wait too much longer or he's gonna start to stink."

The senator regarded us for a moment. His voice was even as he spoke next. "I haven't heard anything from Spero or the others. What happened?"

"Hell if I know, man." Jack appeared agitated at the question. "Like I said, he took off with Reynard. McGinnis was with him. They'd been inside after the dirty work was done. Who knows what they might've found or took from in there. All I know is it's not my problem they haven't checked in yet."

Goddard stepped forward. "It absolutely is your problem. You were the last ones to see him alive and now he's not answering my calls? It doesn't look good, Jack."

Sadie took on a pleading tone. "I saw them leave, too. They just drove off without a word. I don't know what happened."

"Who took Nicolás down?"

"Spero did," I said. "We were supposed to do it as a team, but I got hung up around back and they entered the house before I did. I didn't make it inside until it was all over."

"You were meant to be with him, Michelle. And you, Jack, to keep her safe. So what happened when Spero and the others entered the room?"

Sadie and Jack exchanged a look. She spoke first. "Spero took him upstairs. Told us to wait there. I heard screaming, and then just... nothing. When he came back down he looked agitated. Reynard was injured. They didn't even say anything. They just left."

"And why do you think that is?" Goddard's voice was cold.

Sadie looked nervous. "I really don't know. Did Nicolás have any information that Spero wanted? Did he have a reason to just abandon you like that?"

Instead of answering, Goddard turned to two of his men. "Start at Nicolás's compound and go from there. I want them found before the day is over." He turned to the rest of his guys. "Get Nicolás's body out of the trunk and bring him around back."

With that, Goddard walked back inside and slammed the door. The two men instructed to go after Spero headed to one of the vehicles parked out front. A beefy man with a mustache gestured at Sadie's car with his AR-15 and forced us to the lead the way to the trunk. The remaining three men followed behind. They appeared to be unarmed.

Jack dragged his feet as he made his way over to the Camry. He started making small talk with me, waiting for the other car to pull out of the driveway and disappear down the road.

"I can't wait to get the hell out of this country."

Sadie caught on quickly. "It's not so bad. There are some perks."

"Few and far between" I said. "I miss cheeseburgers."

"You know we have cheeseburgers in Costa Rica, right?" she asked.

I waved my hand. "Don't taste the same."

"You're so full of shit."

"I just have distinguished taste buds."

The beefy guy cut the rifle's barrel between us. "Get on with it."

We'd reached the trunk. Sadie patted her pockets but came up empty-handed for the keys. She looked at Jack. He patted his own pockets, then held up a finger and jogged around to the driver's side of the car. As he popped his head inside, I peeked at the car retreating down the driveway. Just a few more moments and they'd be out of sight.

Jack dug around inside the car for long enough that one of the men got antsy and walked over to the passenger side and stooped to look in the window. Jack popped up and held the dangling keys in his hand.

"Let's go, let's go." The lead man made a sweeping gesture with his rifle.

"Relax, dude. He's not getting any deader." Jack circled back around to the trunk. He stole a glance at the car on its way out as he did. Its taillights faded as it turned the final corner in the driveway. Jack stuck the keys in the trunk and twisted. I felt Sadie tense next to me, ready for what was going to become a fist fight if we were lucky and a massacre if we weren't.

Jack threw open the trunk, dropped his hand inside and spun toward the man with the rifle. He slammed the business end of a baseball bat across the guy's face. The man took it with a grunt and stumbled backward, throwing his hands up in defense a few seconds too late.

A tall, lanky man lunged for Sadie just as she brought her foot up to kick him in the gut. He dropped to his hands and knees. She drove her foot into his face. His head snapped back. Blood poured from his nose.

The remaining two men stalked toward me as I backed around the Camry, drawing them away from the others, hoping the separation would work in our favor.

That's what happened when you were the biggest guy in the room—you got the most attention. While Jack and Sadie had enough of a fight on their hands going one-on-one, I'd have to play it smart by taking on the last two guys from Goddard's team.

These weren't rookies either. They both came at me at the same time swinging. I threw my hands up to block, but immediately took a fist to the stomach. It only slightly knocked the air out of me, but it was enough to catch me off guard. The man on the left, who had long hair and was wearing a beret like some Che Guevara wannabe, pulled out a baton and brought it down on my raised arm. I gritted my teeth against the pain.

One perk of being the biggest guy in the room was intimidation. I could tell the other guy, who seemed to have been trained as a boxer and didn't much use his legs, was playing it safe. His fists packed a wicked punch, but he knew that if I got a good jab in, he'd hit the ground like a ton of bricks. Worse for him was that he had to get close to deliver a strike, increasing the chances I'd connect on a counter.

I backed up until we were at the front end of the car. It smelled like burnt oil and antifreeze. The sounds of blows landing on the other side was nearly enough to distract me. I wanted to make sure Jack and Sadie were handling their own, but one wrong move here and I'd be down for the count.

As soon as I turned the corner of the car, I charged the boxer knowing Che Guevara would be able to land a couple of hits with his baton before I'd be able to turn my full attention to him. I deflected two punches as I moved in close. I picked up the boxer by the waist and slammed him down on the hood of the car driving my shoulder into his gut. The other guy smacked me twice on the back of the head. Black spots exploded in front of me reducing my field of vision in half.

The boxer didn't have room to evade. He was an easy target. He threw up his hands to block my blows, but I pushed through his defenses until my fist connected with his face. A couple of hits later he was a bloody mess, as still as a corpse across the front of the Camry. I endured a few blows across the back from the other man but it was nothing I couldn't wait until later to worry about.

When I spun to face Che Guevara, I had just enough time to lean back and avoid the full force of the end of his baton across my face. But I hadn't moved quickly enough. The tip of his weapon broke open my left cheek and I felt warm blood spill down my face.

My opponent crouched to keep his center of gravity low. If I charged him now he'd be able to use my momentum against me. So I hung back, waited for him to get impatient. Didn't take long. He took two loping steps forward and brought his weapon down aiming for my head again. I was still dizzy from the last hit. If he landed this one I'd probably be out of commission.

I've had my fair share of concussions and I didn't care to add another to my chart.

I threw up my arm to block the blow. The stick smacked my bruised arm. I growled in pain. My anger fueled my strength. I grabbed his wrist and twisted until it popped. He cried out and struggled to pull away. I wrenched the baton from his grasp and whipped him across the face. Blood sprayed from his mouth. The force of the blow spun him around. He collapsed on the ground in a cloud of dirt. Before he had time to recover, I was on him, choking him with the baton against his throat until his body went still.

Breathless, I stood and turned back to the others. I saw Jack standing over his opponent's lifeless body. Sadie had a gash across her arm to rival the one on Jack's side. She'd wrested the knife free from her guy. It now protruded from his chest.

"All right." Jack dusted the dirt from his pants. "Who's up for round two?"

CHAPTER THIRTY

The dust that lined Sadie's nose tickled the back of her throat. She pinched her nostrils together to stifle a sneeze as Jack checked the wound on her arm. She'd told him it wasn't deep enough to worry about. He ignored her. Of course. He was an arrogant son of a bitch. But they worked well together, she thought as she glanced around at the carnage on the ground.

Sunlight reflected off the windows stretching across the front of Goddard's house. She shielded her eyes in an attempt to see what was going on inside.

Jack ripped off a piece of his shirt and wrapped it tightly around her upper bicep. She nodded her thanks, then scooped up the Glock that had been taken from her. Jack found the big guard's rifle, and Bear took the AR-15 he'd placed under the backseat of the car.

She noticed Jack following her stare toward the house.

"He knows we're coming for him," Jack said.

"Probably." Sadie tucked stray strands of hair behind her ear to keep them out of her eyes. "If he didn't watch the fight go down just now, he probably knew the minute we said Spero had run off."

"I'd hoped there was some tension between them that gave Goddard reason to doubt him."

"Minimal. Spero's loyal. He didn't always agree with Goddard, and he didn't always keep his mouth shut about it, but he was here on Goddard's dime. From what I knew about him he wasn't going to throw away that opportunity for his pride."

"The power of the almighty dollar, I suppose."

Bear started toward the house. "We going in through the house or around back?"

"What do you think, big man?"

Bear's tactical brain kicked on. "Smartest thing to do would be to split up. You and Sadie go around back. Confront Goddard. Keep him busy. Try not to get killed. I'll head inside, take out whoever's left. Set myself up in a high window and make sure Goddard doesn't get a chance to try anything smart."

Sadie exchanged a look with Jack. She wished they had Javier's men on their side right about now. But there was no time to call them in. They couldn't wait any longer. The time was now.

"Sounds good to me." Jack started off for the side of the house.

Bear nodded and stayed low as he charged toward the front of the door. He moved with grace and agility. Shocking considering his size. He was through the entrance with minimal commotion.

Sadie followed Jack around the side of the house. The manicured shrubs and trees provided plenty of cover, but that worked both ways. Where they could jump from bush to bush, making sure they weren't seen by any patrolmen, those same men could be lying in wait for them. The pair crept forward slowly and deliberately, ears perked for any snapping branches or rustling leaves.

Halfway down the side of the house, Jack stepped back and pushed Sadie into the bushes. She clamped her mouth shut so she wouldn't cry out in pain as a sharp branch scraped against her injured arm. She glared at Jack fighting against the urge to unleash the stream of profanities that she screamed inside her head.

Jack held a finger to his lips then pointed ahead of them. A pair of men were jogging around the side of the house, presumably to find out what was taking the other team so long to bring the body to Goddard. Jack locked eyes with Sadie. She nodded, acknowledging in that silent glance that she'd follow his lead.

When the men were a few feet from the hiding spot Jack stepped out and clotheslined one of the guards with the end of his rifle as though he were swinging for the fences. The man let out a gargled scream as he fell back to the ground.

Sadie popped out and slammed her foot into the other guy's groin. He bowed forward and she teed off on his face. Two quick blows sent him over to the side, his hands wrapped around his shriveled testicles.

Both Jack and Sadie aimed their firearms at the men's heads. When Jack didn't pull the trigger, she looked up. He was peering off into the distance.

"We gotta keep quiet," he said. "Maybe we can get the jump on Goddard."

Sadie looked down at her target. "Works for me." She raised her weapon and smacked the man in the temple. His eyes shut and his body settled back just as Jack did the same to the other guy. They dragged them into the bushes and continued down the side of the house.

When they reached the corner the pair stuck as close to the siding as possible. They took a moment to catch their breath and listened for any clues as to what was going on out back. They locked eyes after a minute. Sadie nodded to indicate she was ready. Jack nodded back and eased around the corner in an attempt to get a lay of the land before they charged forward.

Sadie sensed something was wrong even before she realized that Jack had frozen in place instead of leaning back so he wouldn't be seen. His body went rigid. Hers mimicked his despite not knowing the source of his shock. That didn't last long. Jack dropped his rifle and stepped away from the corner of the house. Then a voice filled the air.

"You can come out, Michelle. I know you're there." It was Goddard. He sounded far away as though he was shouting across the lawn.

Sadie stepped up behind Jack. Her gaze narrowed in on the man who held a silver revolver with an eight-inch barrel to Jack's head. She recognized him as one of Goddard's trusted bodyguards. He was always nameless. Probably preferred it that way. Perhaps he would be the guy who would take over Spero's position if things worked out in their favor.

Don't get your hopes up, bud.

"Bring them around," Goddard called out.

The man took a couple steps back and gestured with his revolver. Jack and Sadie stepped around him into the backyard. A sprawling lawn stretched to the flowing river with hedges and flowerbeds placed strategically throughout. Goddard sat with his right leg crossed over the other. An orange umbrella covered the small circular table. A sweating pitcher of water sat in the middle alongside three empty glasses. Goddard sipped from a fourth.

Two men dressed in black pants and shirts watched the back door to the house. Sadie didn't recognize them. There were usually different men at the house. Guys Goddard hired on a per diem basis. Another guard stood behind Goddard with his rifle at the ready. Despite the standoff and Sadie's betrayal, the senator sat there with a smile on his face as he traced lines in the condensation rings left behind by his glass. There was a manic gleam to his eye.

"I really should've known better, right, Jack?"

"You really should've," Jack said. "Christ, with the amount of time you spend with those slimeballs—" Jack held up a finger, "—I'm sorry, your fellow politicians, you'd think you could spot a snake in the grass."

Goddard's smile spread, he turned to Sadie. "You were the biggest surprise of all, my dear. Everything we'd gone through over the years. Did it mean nothing? How could you betray me for an old friend?"

Sadie shook her head. "Jack? I barely know the guy. It's been, what, a couple of days?"

Jack counted on his fingers. "Sounds about right."

Goddard's grin finally dimmed. Sadie reveled in the shock on his face.

"You didn't figure that part out yet? The part where it really did mean nothing to me. How does it feel knowing you'd been played since the day I came into your life?"

Goddard rose quickly, his knee catching the edge of the table. It tilted to the other side then crashed back down. The water inside the pitcher splashed onto the table, but the senator paid no mind.

"You're lying."

"I can get my creds for you. Or maybe I'll call Langley and you can verify with my handler."

"Handler?" Goddard grabbed the back of his chair and steadied himself. The weight of the situation fell upon his shoulders. The CIA had been onto him, watching him, for years now. There would be no escaping this situation.

Jack stepped forward. He paid for the advance when that long revolver smashed against the back of his head. His legs went out from under him and he collapsed to his right knee. He grimaced and sucked in a long breath of air to counter the pain and clear his mind. The jolt radiated across his head and down his neck. "As fun as it is to see you processing all of this, Senator, I have to say we're on a bit of a time crunch." Like a boxer in his last heavyweight fight, Jack forced himself back to his feet to take another swing. "You've got no more moves left. Give it up."

"I can still have my guys put a bullet in your brain."

Jack shrugged off Goddard's threat. "You can. But then you're killing a federal agent, and you're not getting out of here any time soon. The CIA has a folder for you. Other agencies do, too. You think you're gonna beat this? No government is gonna harbor you. Your career is over. Your life is over."

"Then what's the point of drawing this out."

Sadie saw Goddard's gaze slide to the right. He gave a curt nod. There was a moment's hesitation and then thunder cracked the air. She flinched, fearing another round would explode from the revolver meant for her.

Except it didn't come from behind her.

The shot rang out from two floors up.

Behind her a body hit the ground. There was another shot. The man to the side fell. Before she turned back, another pop sounded and the guard behind Goddard fell.

Jack grabbed the revolver from the dead guy and aimed it the two sentries posted by the back door. In the confusion of the moment they hadn't moved.

Goddard froze in place. A span of ten seconds passed. He charged back under the umbrella. He was as good as dead, but he was correctly banking on the fact that they didn't want to kill him just yet.

Sadie scanned the second-floor windows and spotted the barrel of Bear's AR-15 resting on the sill. From that vantage point, he couldn't hit the two men stationed outside the door.

"One of you take him out!" Goddard shouted. The one on the right turned and ran inside.

Sadie called out to warn Bear.

The other guard raised his weapon, but before he could take aim his body jerked three times, coinciding with the three shots Jack fired into the man's chest. He fell backward, crashing through the French door.

Jack stalked toward the senator, revolver raised. He paused long enough to see how Goddard would react. The politician was just that; he was no soldier, no hero, but he stood his ground nonetheless. Jack lowered his pistol and stepped up to him, eye-to-eye, toe-to-toe.

Thomas Goddard didn't shrink.

So Jack pistol whipped him across the face and brought the man to his knees. He took a step back and aimed at Goddard's forehead.

"The point of drawing this out, Senator," Jack said, "is because we have a few matters to discuss before I blow your skull off."

CHAPTER THIRTY-ONE

The ringing in my ears persisted for several seconds following the shots. I spotted Sadie on the lawn. She was warning me about an incoming guard. Son of a bitch should've known better after what had happened moments ago.

The door stood open to the quiet house. The buzzing subsided second by second. Through the open window I heard three gunshots, followed by a dull thud and then Jack talking to Goddard.

Inside the man thundered up the stairs as though he were trying to win a race. He stopped at the landing, heaving heavily in an attempt to catch his breath. There was a *chink-chink* sound as he racked his pistol's slide.

I backed into the corner, out of view. Pulled the rifle up and zeroed in a few inches in front of the doorway. There was no reason to do it quietly. But it'd be quick. One bullet to his head.

He shoved his arm into the room, but his aim was off. I steadied my breathing, long and slow. My finger rested on the trigger. Beads of sweat slipped from my hairline. I resisted the urge to wipe my fore-head. His foot breached the threshold, then his torso, and finally his head. He caught sight of me out of the corner of his eye. A second later I put a bullet through it.

I grabbed his shotgun, left the room and descended the stairs. The drone in my ears made keeping myself tuned into any little sounds a challenge. A quick scan revealed that the rest of the house appeared empty, but something pulled at me and gave me reason to pause. There had been plenty of men guarding the house, but something still seemed to be missing. As I hit the ground floor I paused with my hand on the banister. Goddard was never on his own, but that didn't necessarily mean his guards were always present.

He had a very dedicated personal assistant who was always at his side.

I recalled the guy named Jordan. PDA in hand, Jordan had never been more than a few feet away from his boss. So where was he now? I closed my eyes to better tune into my surroundings. The house groaned and creaked and popped. It was a large structure and the rising temperatures would have that effect on it. But it wouldn't cause the floorboards to creak in quick succession, as if someone were hurrying across them to get to the front door.

My eyes flew open and I launched myself forward, skidding to a halt in the foyer the second Jordan had entered from another direction. He cried out and tried to turn the other way, but his momentum threw his feet out from under him and he slipped and crashed to his knees. His ever-present PDA went skidding across marble floor and bounced off the wall. A spider web of tiny cracks covered the screen.

I grabbed it from the ground with one hand. The other gripped Jordan by the back of the collar and hauled him to his feet. He was so light he actually went airborne for a few seconds. His legs went weak and he couldn't stand on his own. I dragged him along with me toward the back of the house.

Jordan gasped at the sight of the dead guard at the exit. I kicked the remaining French door open, threw the man outside. He skipped along the concrete like a smooth stone on water.

Jack stood in front of Goddard, his pistol trained on the man. He raised his free hand and pointed at me. "All good in there?"

"Yeah," I said. "Found this little weasel trying to sneak out."

Jack nodded. The tension in his face eased. His lips twitched into a half smile, which faded almost as soon as it formed.

This was our mission and it was finally coming to a close.

I grabbed Jordan by his mane and crossed the grass. I tossed the man down next to his boss and placed the PDA on the table. A glass of water waited there. I downed it in three gulps then poured another and polished it off.

"Keep an eye out," Jack said.

I took a moment to take in the scene before me. Goddard was on his knees, sweat tracking down his temples, gun to his head, fear in his eyes.

"What do you want?" Goddard asked.

"What's your passion, Senator?"

"Excuse me?"

"It's a fairly straightforward question. What's your passion? I like to travel. I can't stay in one place for too long. I get antsy. I'm not a very nice person when I get antsy." Jack turned to me. "What's your passion, Bear?"

I didn't miss a beat. "Steak and beer."

"See, Senator? Easy question. What's your passion?"

"Helping the American people and—"

The giant revolver cracked through the relative silence. Jack put a bullet three inches to the right of the senator's knee. It left a hole in the ground an anaconda could've slithered through. Goddard flinched, tears tracked down his face. He must've thought he was above something like this ever happening to him. Jordan was shaking uncontrollably. Jack moved the gun back to point at Goddard's head. "Cut the bullshit. What are you working on back home? What's your passion project?"

He took a few shaky breaths, exhaled loudly. "I-I'm working on a pipeline project." When his words were met with a blank stare, he continued. "It would carry oil down from Canada into the Mid-West. I've been getting a lot of push back from other members of Congress, but we're on the verge of getting the last holdouts to sign up."

"You blackmailing people into voting yes?"

Goddard shifted uncomfortably.

"Don't lie to me, man. It won't end well for you."

"Yes." Goddard closed his eyes and took a deep breath. When he opened them again, I could see the cogs starting to spin. "It's going to go through. It's going to bring thousands of jobs to America. It's going to make us less dependent on the Middle East."

Sadie crossed her arms. "How safe is it?"

Goddard's silence was response enough.

I turned to Jack. "Same old shit, man. Either side of the aisle, It's all about the money. Who cares who gets screwed over in the meantime."

Jack chewed his lip. "You think this is it? You think this is what Thorne has his eye on? If Goddard's death gets back to the U.S. before the pipeline gets the go-ahead, all those people he blackmailed will be off the hook. Why does Thorne want it to go through so badly? What does he get out of it?"

"Who's Thorne?" Goddard asked.

"Someone who likes you even less than we do, apparently. Only he's not getting a paycheck to put you in the ground."

Goddard's eyes lit up with a renewed sense of hope. "I can pay you. Let me go, tell them you killed me, and I'll double whatever you're pulling in now."

Jordan looked over at his boss. He had a look on his face that said he believed the man could save them.

Jack lowered the revolver. When a smile spread across the senator's face, Jack shook his head. "You're going to die. Just not by my hand."

When Jack held the firearm out to his side, Sadie stepped forward and grabbed it from him, then walked up to Goddard, stopping a few feet short. She aimed at his head. The barrel was so long it was dangerously close to Goddard's reach. No one missed the flash of anger in his eyes.

"I spent a long time dreaming about this day, Thomas. The Agency shackled me, though. The mission was superior to morals."

"You bitch." He spat in her direction but the glob of saliva made it about an inch past his lips before diving and crashing on his chest.

"I've seen the things you've done," she said. "Trust me, this is a mercy."

"I never pulled a trigger." He sliced his hands out in front of him. "I never killed anyone."

Sadie didn't budge. "You might've never pulled a trigger, but you've killed plenty of people, Senator. I've got the numbers. I've got the evidence. I could put you away for a thousand years with as much as I've gathered on you."

"So why don't you?"

"You'd find a way to worm your way out of it." Sadie widened her stance and tightened her grip on the revolver. "Besides, some people just don't deserve a second chance."

When the shot rang out Jack and I didn't flinch. The tension eased out of Sadie's shoulders. The bullet went in between Goddard's eyes and took the back of his head off as it exited. She lowered the gun only after the senator's body fell back and hit the ground.

Jack approached her from the side. He reached for the revolver. She gave it up without a fight. He put his hand on her shoulder. "You all right?"

Sadie took a minute to answer. Her voice was steady when she did. "I'm angry that all the people he hurt over the years won't get the retribution they deserve." She looked up at Jack. "But yeah. I'm okay."

I walked across the grass and stopped in front of Jordan. He'd soiled his pants somewhere along the way. He was shaking, tears streamed down his face. He managed to look me in the eye. "And what should we do with this one?"

Jack and Sadie exchanged a look. We were all thinking the same thing. He had been with Goddard the whole time. He had been privy to the senator's every move. He was as much a culprit as his boss had been.

"I can tell you all about the pipeline." Jordan fought through his cracking voice. "I can tell you who's involved in it. I can tell you what else Goddard was into and who he was working with. I've got names. Evidence. Congressmen who would be none too happy if they knew Goddard had kept a record of their indiscretions."

I looked to Jack. Jordan wasn't on the hit list, and he might have some value to the Feds back home. "What do you think, partner?"

Jack kept his focus on Jordan. "I think I need some answers. You stay useful, you'll stay alive."

No sooner had Jack finished his sentence than his phone buzzed in his pocket. He fished it out and swore. It was Vasquez. He put it up to his ear. "What?" There was a pause. Jack's face twisted in anger. "It's done. Now tell us where the girl is."

I couldn't hear what Vasquez was saying, but I had an idea. Even if he told us Camila's location, it would allow him to be long gone before we could do anything about bringing him in or giving him the same fate as Goddard.

Jack's grip on the phone tightened. "I can't wait until the day we meet again, Vasquez. One of us won't walk away from that meeting."

Vasquez said something else before hanging up, that caused Jack to nearly throw the phone at the house. He turned toward us. He held the revolver in front of his face, shaking it.

"What is it?" Sadie said.

"I know where Camila is."

CHAPTER THIRTY-TWO

The four of us stopped in front of Sadie's car. Vultures circled overhead, casting shadows on the bodies that littered the ground. The corpses already started to swell and the smell of human excrement was strong.

Jordan stopped and bent over and threw up all over his feet. He rose, shaking, and wiped his mouth. He tried to make himself small after, perhaps hoping he wouldn't be noticed. I didn't think we'd have any issues with him, but I kept a wary look out anyway. If he managed to escape, we might not learn what Thorne was up to. Besides, the kind of information Jordan had was a special type of currency. I'd rather be holding that in my hand than see it in someone else's.

I tossed the little guy in the backseat, then climbed in after him. Jack and Sadie took their positions in the front. She turned the key in the ignition. The engine stuttered a few seconds then came to life. Sadie adjusted the vents after cranking the air on high. She held her hand there for a moment, then shook her head as she cut the fan off.

Jack turned to her. He jutted his chin toward Jordan. "I need you to take him to Javier. Keep him safe. Make sure no one informs Frank. I don't want him or anyone else in on this until we know what we're dealing with concerning Thorne."

"What are you going to do?" she asked.

Jack glanced over his shoulder at me. "We're going after Vasquez."

"What about Camila?" Sadie gripped the wheel. She'd left the car in park and pressed angrily against the gas pedal. The engine wailed in response and the car shook. "We can't leave her."

Jack placed his hand on her arm. "I never said we were going to. Meet up with Javier. Hand over Jordan." Jack popped the glove compartment and pulled out a crumbled napkin and a chewed-up pen. He wrote down an address and handed it to her. "Then tell Javier he'll find his daughter at this location."

I leaned forward until I was in between them. "How do you know we can trust this guy? I mean, look at everything he put us through."

"He doesn't want to hurt that little girl." Jack eased back against the door and placed a hand over his eyes. "Call it instinct, or a hunch, but I can hear it in his voice. He saw an opportunity and he begrudgingly took it. The girl served her purpose. Vasquez has a granddaughter about the same age. He wouldn't be able to hurt Camila any more than he'd be able to hurt his own."

"And what are you two going to do?" Sadie asked.

Jack tossed the pen back into the glove compartment and snapped the door shut. "Like I said, we're going after Vasquez."

"You gonna look at him down the barrel of your gun?" I asked. "No one's gonna back us up if you do."

Jack again shifted in his seat so that our three faces were inches apart. "That all depends on one thing."

Sadie and I were silent as we waited for Jack to finish his thought. When he didn't, Sadie asked, "And that is?"

"How useful he can be to me."

SADIE DROPPED US OFF AT THE LAND ROVER AND JACK HOPPED into the front seat. He pulled Thorne's shades down over his eyes, which served as a reminder of the fire we were heading into. Vasquez was a pit stop on the way back home, on the way back to Frank, and on the way to figuring out what the hell Thorne was up to.

Before exiting the Camry I secured Jordan with a length of rope and jumper cables Sadie kept in the trunk of her car. It was too hot to throw him back there, so I laid him down on the back seat with a threat that I'd castrate him if he caused her any trouble. The tears in his eyes indicated he took me seriously.

I settled into the Land Rover's passenger's seat and leaned it back as far is it could go. It was hot. I was covered in dirt and blood and sweat. The damn air conditioning didn't work in this car either. I could've used a nap, but I doubted my near-constant state of adrenaline these past few days would allow me to get more than a couple winks. In fact, it might dull my edge, so I scrapped the idea altogether.

A few minutes after Jack had pulled away from the curb, I spoke up. "So where are we heading?"

"The airport."

I looked down at myself, then at him. "The airport? You seen us lately? We're not getting through any kind of security check like this."

Jack drummed his fingers against the wheel. His mood was continuously rising. There was no music playing, but he didn't seem to notice. "So we'll stop then." He paused a few beats. "After all of this, after seeing Camila and finally turning her over to Javier, what do you think is the first thing Vasquez will want to do?"

"See his family."

"Exactly."

"But the airport? Why do you suppose he's gonna fly out of here?"

"Vasquez is smart. And he understands that distance is a good thing. He would never keep his family in the same city where he does business. The trick is figuring out where he's flying to."

"International or domestic?"

Jack nodded. "Would he keep his family in the same country in case something came up? If they're close enough, he can jump on a small charter plane and take care of any problems. If they're back in the States, back in Miami, they'd be far enough away that few people would be able to use them as leverage."

"But then he'd run into the issue of trusting other people with his family's safety."

"I imagine Vasquez has a wide network of friends." He thought for a moment. "Enemies, too, for that matter. But how many of his associates would he trust with his family's lives?"

"Vasquez was a cop. Those guys bond for life. If anyone followed him from that life into this one, that would be enough to trust them with something that important."

The wind rush streaming in through the open window blew Jack's hair back. "Vasquez would use his old connections, the ones who looked the other way when it came to his new occupation. That's who would protect his family."

"That still doesn't answer where they are, though. Even if we know they're back in the U.S.—hell, even if we know they're in Miami—that's a pretty big area to search."

Jack pressed his foot to the gas a little harder. From my view it looked as though we were doing twenty over the speed limit. He braked and turned into a small parking lot, pointing at a clothing store. "Which is why we need to get to the airport before he takes off. So let's hurry up here."

We headed inside, found the restrooms and washed the muck off our hands, arms and faces. Then we each grabbed a pair of khaki pants, and button-up shirts. The kind tourists like to wear with lots of flowers and junk on them.

"To the airport," Jack said once we were seated in the car again.

"This is a risk, man. We need a backup plan."

"I've got one." Jack reached behind him and grabbed Jordan's PDA off the bench seat. I had noticed it back there when we got into the car but had figured he planned on turning it over at some point so the data could be extracted. The screen was smashed and it was probably password protected.

I looked up at him when he handed it over to me. "How is this going to help?"

Jack grinned at me. "I had our friend Jordan bring up everything on Vasquez before we parted ways."

"It didn't take me that long to take a piss, man."

Jack laughed. His mood was starting to improve mine. "Only took a couple of seconds. Go ahead. Unlock it. See what we're working with."

I swiped at the screen. My skin caught on the jagged glass in a couple spots. Despite its condition, the device worked without a glitch. When the lock screen faded away, a detailed spreadsheet took its place. It took me a minute to take in all the information.

"Holy shit."

"I'm thinking of hiring Jordan as my personal assistant," Jack said. "He's nothing if not thorough."

I read off the top row of the spreadsheet. "Date, To, From, Location, Time Stamp, Receipts." I looked up. "Goddard knew how much Vasquez spent on his morning coffee every day and whether or not he decided to put sugar in it that day."

"And Vasquez thought he was the private investigator. I'm telling you, I think Jordan has a future in espionage if he wants it. I'm gonna recommend to Frank that he needs to take this guy, lock him up in a cell with a computer and put him to work."

I waved off his babbling. "There are several entries here for flights back to Miami."

"Doesn't mean his family is there." Jack paused while he took a sharp right turn. When we straightened out, he checked his rearview and continued. "It'd make sense for him to make a lot of trips back to his former stomping ground, especially if he's got contacts back there who can help him with deals in Costa Rica and elsewhere."

"But a lot of these receipts once he lands are for toys and children's clothes."

Jack cracked another smile. "Exactly. It'd take some time, but we'd be able to figure out where his family lives now."

"But we're not ones to mess with other people's kids and grand-kids like that. No matter what they've done or how bad they are. So what's the play here?"

Jack's smile faded and he turned his head toward me. "Vasquez turned on Goddard because his hand was too obvious. He directly threatened Vasquez's family. I don't have any interest in doing that and I don't think it would work out in our favor."

"But?"

"But showing up at the airport means we're close. We don't need to say we know where his family is. Even if he assumes we don't have an address, he's going to be cautious. He's going to be more cooperative."

"Or more hostile."

Jack shrugged. "A man like Vasquez didn't get to where he is today by having a temper. His revenge on Goddard was clinical. There may have been emotion behind the decision, but everything after that was a strategic move on the chess board. Look at how he handled us. He's gonna keep his cool so long as we play it calm. All we wanna do is talk."

"About what? How is Vasquez going to be useful to us now? Goddard's dead. Chances Vasquez has connections with Skinner is pretty slim."

"Our new friend Jordan may be good at doing the leg work, but Vasquez has connections. He knows how to find information when no one else can. And I think he's smart enough to realize that if he helps us, he's expanding his network, both with us and with Frank."

"And you really think he's gonna buy that we're cool as cucumbers now after what just happened?"

"It's just business. Right?"

I shrugged. "Not so sure about that. Anyway, you think he's gonna help us figure out what's going on with Thorne?"

"Even better." Jack turned to me and waited until I met his gaze. "He's gonna help us beat Thorne at his own game."

CHAPTER THIRTY-THREE

Wild vines climbed the three-story office building. Grass grew through cracks in the deserted parking lot. The place had been abandoned for years, Javier had said. Sadie believed it. The afternoon sun hovered over the tree line. There was no breeze here, making it feel even hotter and more stifling than earlier. She could smell the effect the day had had on her and hoped the ordeal would be over soon so she could get out of her clothes and under a cool stream of water. One that could wash the past few days away.

Javier had resisted the idea of sending his men into the building without him. His daughter was within reach now, but protocol required he stayed behind. It took Sadie and his right-hand man, Rafael Calderon, to convince him to stay put. He had plenty of men at his disposal. Let them go in and make sure the building was clear. They would react to any potential scenario as they had been trained. They'd do it without the emotion that Javier was drowning in. God forbid something did happen. The man wouldn't be in any kind of condition to make the calls. It was a good thing his second-in-charge was present. Sadie didn't want to have to do it, though she'd accept the responsibility if required.

Sadie had also argued to keep Javier on the sidelines because she had no idea how he'd react to seeing his daughter, dead or alive. Vasquez was a wild card to her and she didn't share Jack's full faith that the guy wouldn't harm Camila. But she agreed that Javier was never the target. It had always been Goddard.

A means to an end.

Camila's condition aside, they didn't know what they were walking into. What if there were men in there? Explosives? Some kind of trap? What if Vasquez feared retribution for his part in this? There was no guarantee they would allow Vasquez to get away with kidnapping and holding his daughter hostage.

Javier wore a path in the asphalt behind Sadie. His footsteps echoed through their silent surroundings. She kept her focus on the door to the building and double checked her comms unit. She had learned a few minutes prior that Vasquez owned a shell corporation that had bought the building and kept it standing for private meetings and brokered its use out when groups needed a large area to load and unload merchandise. She suspected it had a few other uses, too.

The team Javier had sent ahead was lined up against the façade of the building. There were six total, clad in tactical gear, ready to breech the front door. The first man tested the handle and then swung the door inward. When nothing happened, he signaled for his team to follow him and the men filed inside, their H&K MP5s at the ready.

A solid five minutes passed before they received an update from the team. Javier double-timed his pacing. His collar was soaked with sweat. It coated his face, arms, and his hair had grown slick with it. His shoulders were high and tense. He balled his fists. The muscles on his forearms ripped. Veins poked out. The world around them was silent. Sadie would've killed for an update. An all-clear would've been even more welcome.

Sadie no sooner had the thought than her phone buzzed in her hand. Javier was by her side before she even lifted it to her ear. It smelled like he hadn't showered in a couple days. She put a calming hand on his shoulder and pushed him back as she listened to Rafael Calderon's voice over the line.

"We're on the third floor. No souls on the first two. We found his daughter. Tell him she's alive."

She didn't have to. Javier pressed his sweaty body into hers so that he could hear the conversation. His reaction was delayed. He stood there, staring at Sadie for several moments. Then his eyes misted. He sank to his knees and sobbed. Sadie remained where she stood, phone to her ear. She wondered why Calderon had chosen to call rather than use their comms system.

She knew there was something he hadn't said yet.

"We've got a situation."

"What is it?" She looked down at Javier and longed for the unaware bliss he was experiencing.

"There's a bomb strapped to Camila's chest." Sadie could hear someone in the background trying to reassure the girl that everything was going to be okay. "I've got a couple of my guys working on it now."

There was a pause where Sadie could tell Calderon pulled the phone away from his ear and covered the mouthpiece. Why would Vasquez do this? Would he really blow the girl up after all this? Did he have a beef with Javier that she was unaware of? Or was the guy simply trying to buy himself some time to ensure his getaway? She heard incoherent mumbling on the other end before he came back on the line, clear as before.

"She's asking for her father."

Sadie looked down at Javier. The man wasn't bound to react well to the news that his daughter was connected to an explosive, but she didn't feel as though there was any way to avoid it. He deserved to see her and was already climbing to his feet to do just that. He extended his hand. She grabbed it and pulled him close to her. If these were Camila's last minutes on Earth, she should be spending them with her father.

"We're heading in." Sadie hung up the phone. Javier looked at her with wide eyes unable to contain the hurricane of emotion within. She didn't revel in the fact she was the one to relay bad news, but she didn't have a choice. "There's been a complication."

Javier went still. He didn't speak. He didn't have to. The question burned in his eyes.

Sadie decided not to mince words. "There's a bomb. They're working on dismantling it right now, but she's asking for you. She wants you there."

Javier sprinted off toward the front of the building. He had an obvious limp on the left side, as though he'd suffered a traumatic injury there at some point in his life and never fully recovered. But he didn't let up. He had the kind of determination that even a brick wall wouldn't have stopped him.

Sadie signaled for a couple of the remaining men to follow her in and ordered the rest to remain vigilant. The first team had cleared the building. But she hadn't. Measure twice, cut once was the saying, she thought. Human error had resulted in the loss of lives more than once, and in her presence. Considering they were already playing with fire, she wasn't going to take more chances than necessary.

The small contingent jogged to catch up with Javier. By the time they reached the door, the man was already on his way up the first set of stairs, taking three at a time. His footsteps echoed in the empty space. By the time Sadie reached the second landing, Javier was gone.

They reached the third floor. Sadie followed the sounds of a girl and her father's sobs. Low chatter rose to full voices as they traveled down a wide hallway and into the room at the end of the corridor. It opened into a large space with exposed brick columns and boxes stacked haphazardly along the walls. The carpet had been ripped out. Garbage and dust littered the floor. Vasquez had clearly not used the building, or at least this level, for some time.

When Sadie turned the corner, her eyes immediately zeroed in on Javier and Camila. The girl's brown hair was greasy and matted. Dirt and grime coated her face. But her eyes shone brightly against her skin. She was crying as her gaze locked on her father. She didn't seem terrified though. Javier had settled the girl. Whatever happened, they faced it together.

Calderon urged Javier to get back so their men could do their jobs. They were as experienced as any Sadie had met. The device didn't appear to be anything sophisticated, so better to let them work and get this ordeal over with. Javier recognized this. He rose, leaned over, kissed his daughter on the cheek, then took a few steps back.

"I'm here with you," he said. "Right here."

She stared at him, oblivious to the world around her at that moment.

Sadie circled around to the side to better take in the scene. She was in it until the end as well it seemed. Two men worked quickly and cautiously on the vest draped over Camila's chest. They had to disarm it before they could take it off.

Within a few minutes they had freed the girl from the device. The entire room exhaled in relief, watching as the tech carried it out of the room while the other checked Camila's restraints for triggers. Finding none, he cut her free and smiled as she fled to her father.

The pair collapsed into each other's arms and sunk to their knees, crying and laughing and whispering *I love you* over and over again. Some of them turned away from the raw emotion, but Sadie drank it in. This was what she lived for. This was why she had become an agent in the first place. She had done some terrible things for Goddard while undercover, but it had always been with the bigger picture in mind. This right here was what made it all worth it.

The group trickled out of the room, making their way downstairs and outside into sunlight peeking through the trees. It had never felt so warm and comforting. Sadie flipped open her phone and shot a text to Jack.

Camila is safe. Vasquez had planted a bomb on her, but Javier's men dismantled it. They're reunited. All good.

She hit send and watched as the note flitted off. Unable to stop bubbling anger from reaching the surface, she tapped out another message.

Kick his ass for me, will you?

CHAPTER THIRTY-FOUR

I dropped Jack off in front of a couple of tall palm trees. Exhaust-ridden air milled about the Land Rover's cabin. The taste lingered in my mouth and throat even after I swallowed down a mouthful of cola. Jack hopped a guardrail and blended in with a mixed crowd of tourists on their way to the entrance after departing their bus.

The plan was straightforward. We had narrowed down three flights going out of the Juan Santamaría InternationalAirport and heading into Miami. Two of them were on American, the third on United. All left within the next hour or so. If Jack was right about Vasquez, the guy was already at the airport.

Noble's job was to run inside and get a ticket. Any ticket to anywhere using an identity no one knew about. After today he'd have to burn it. With the ticket in hand, he'd have to get through security and track down Vasquez before he boarded his flight. I had a feeling that once the man was gone, he might not come back. Why would he? Chances were Javier would not let this go.

I was tasked with getting Vasquez on the phone to home in on his location. We figured the guy was in the airport, so if we could get some clue from the call, an announcement over the speakers perhaps, we could locate him. I had to keep him on the phone as long as possible.

I dialed the number and put the call on speaker. The wind and sounds of the road would be audible to Vasquez. Which was perfect. I wanted him to know I was in the car, let him think he was safely out of reach behind the security checkpoint.

Vasquez answered on the third fuzzy ring. "Hello, Jack."

"Sorry to disappoint," I said.

"Ah, Riley Logan, I presume? Should I call you Bear?"

"Only my friends call me Bear."

"I'd like to think one day we could potentially be friends, Riley."

"You have a lot to live up to, man. My friends don't kidnap ten-year-old girls."

"We all do what we must," Vasquez said. "Besides, it wasn't me that did the act. Garcia did it. I saved her life."

"You didn't exactly set her free."

"Like I said, we all do what we must. I gave up her location in good faith, trusting that you did, indeed, kill Goddard." He spoke hurriedly. Was he getting ready to board?

"The senator's dead." I swerved to pass an old man driving a large sedan who had stopped in the middle of the road. "We kept our word."

"As did I. Have you tracked her down yet?"

I turned the corner into one of the many parking lots at the airport and began searching for a spot. "They're closing in. Jack had a head start on me. I had some trash to throw out."

"Well, lucky me then." Vasquez paused and the phone amplified the background noise in the airport, though I couldn't make anything out. "I'm a little perplexed at the moment. Tell me, to what do I owe the pleasure of this call?"

"I want to know your plan from here on out."

Vasquez laughed. It sounded genuine to me, as though the man was delighting in the fact that I'd been so upfront with his request. "You know this only works in the movies, right? I'm not going to divulge my secrets to you."

"Not even to a potential friend?"

Vasquez laughed again. "Fair point, fair point." He paused. "But no, Riley. You'd have to earn a little more trust than that."

I located an empty spot and backed in despite the sign saying not to. "Do you honestly think you'll be able to outrun Javier forever? Or that you'll be able to outrun Jack?"

"No," Vasquez said. "But I don't need to. I just—"

He was interrupted by an overhead announcement. A woman's voice rang out in Spanish. *"United customer Rafael Gonzalez please make your way to gate five. That's United customer Rafael Gonzale—."*

Vasquez seemed to realize his mistake a second too late. The line cut out. But I had all the information I needed. I fired off a text to Jack with Vasquez's location. It was only a matter of minutes now.

JACK PURCHASED A TICKET TO LIMON, THEN MADE IT THROUGH security in record time. It helped that he had nothing with him. He emptied his pockets into a small tray and stepped in line to go through the metal detector. He smiled at the woman waving people through and said *gracias* once he was given the all clear.

When he stepped out past security, he had three choices. He could either go left, go right, or stay put. If he walked off in one of the directions, he chanced heading in the wrong one and potentially missing Vasquez if he had to double back and try to catch up with him. Or he might accidentally pass the guy without realizing it, revealing himself in the process. If he stayed put, it meant he could head straight for his target once he heard from Bear, but he still risked not being able to catch up with Vasquez. It also looked suspicious.

In the end, he opted to stay put.

He didn't have to wait long. A text came in from Bear with Vasquez's location. He was flying out United, around gate five. Bear texted that Vasquez had realized his mistake and ended the call prematurely. Would the guy be on the move now? Or trying to board his flight early?

As Jack narrowed in on gate 5 he searched for a man he had only seen for a moment in person and a few times in a grainy photo stashed inside a manila folder. Still, Vasquez wasn't hard to distinguish. He was tall and well-built and carried himself in a manner that said he was above everyone else. Most of the people here were haggard travelers or harried families. Because of how Vasquez carried himself, the oceans of people would part before him. There'd be a ripple effect.

When Jack spotted him, Vasquez was standing outside the restroom. He had his hand on the door and was glancing around. His gaze swept right past Jack without a sign of recognition. Vasquez's plan appeared to be to wait it out inside a stall. There were worse places in the airport, Jack supposed, but he couldn't think of one right off hand.

Vasquez had to be banking that Jack and Bear would canvas the airport, think that they'd missed him, then work back outside. A gamble for sure. Then Jack spotted the second man. Made sense that Vasquez would have a scout positioned to relay movements. The guy was dressed in a pair of tan slacks and a white polo shirt. He leaned against the wall outside the bathroom, his head tilted down at the phone in his hand. But his eyes which were no longer hidden by his glasses darted side to side. They were always on the move scanning the space.

Jack found a small store a few kiosks down from gate five. The place was crammed with newspapers, magazines, and paperbacks, as well as souvenir shirts and hats. He purchased a cap and put it on and folded the bag and tucked it in his pocket. He only had to wait a few minutes before a fresh wave of new arrivals filled the area, walking off in every direction. Naturally a large group of them headed for the restrooms. Jack found his way to the middle and kept his head down and his phone to his ear. The man outside the bathroom looked up and scanned the group. From under his ball cap, Jack watched. Their gazes never met. He managed to slide right past the lookout undetected.

Inside the bathroom Jack went to the row of sinks. He used the mirrors to check the handful of stalls behind him. Each one of them was occupied. Wrinkled shorts and pants sat down around the occupants' ankles atop tennis shoes, sandals, flip flops, and one pair of freshly shined black oxfords.

That was his man.

He washed his hands, spent some time at a urinal, washed his hands again. He took off his hat and fixed his hair. He blew his nose. It took a few minutes, but the lull that always arrives finally arrived. They were alone. Jack figured that the guy outside would've been tasked with keeping track of how many people had come and gone. Apparently not, though.

Jack pushed open a stall door with the back of his hand and stepped inside. He'd already grown accustom to the smell in the room, so waiting out Vasquez wouldn't be that big of a deal. He watched the other stall in the mirror through a crack in the rusted door.

He pulled his buzzing phone from his pocket. It was a message from Sadie. Before he could open it, another message hit his phone. Camila was safe. The op didn't go down as smoothly as they had hoped. The asshole in the stall next door had strapped a bomb to the girl's chest. He'd pay for that. Jack let out a relieved sigh. Perhaps Vasquez thought it was for natural reasons, unaware that Jack had entered his flow state. He no longer had to hold back.

A few seconds later a toilet flushed, a man rose, pulled up his pants, and unlatched his stall door. Jack watched as it swung open slowly and Vasquez emerged into the empty bank of sinks.

Jack was sitting patiently, not even bothered by the fact he was stuck in a men's restroom at an airport in San José. He was riding the high that was the image of him punching Vasquez in the face.

A stream of water flowed over Vasquez's hands. He washed, rinsed, then cupped them and splashed the liquid over his face. He only recognized his mistake a few moments later when he started blindly searching for something to dry his eyes with.

Jack opened his door and slid up to the man just as Vasquez pulled his shirt up to his face and patted the water away. He dropped his shirt. His eyes moved to Jack's reflection. Vasquez's body stiffened.

Jack moved to block his exit. He held his arms loose at his side, ready for an attack. He was close enough to the guy to disarm him should he pull a weapon, and far enough away to avoid a strike.

He said, "I wouldn't try it if I were you."

Vasquez said, "What do you want from me? I thought we were done."

"We would've been, but you decided to put a bomb on a kid."

Vasquez clenched his jaw. "That was to buy time only. Surely by now Javier's men have determined the explosives were duds. Nothing was going to happen. I even told the girl that myself."

Jack sized the guy up. Maybe he was telling the truth. It didn't matter. "You know, for some reason I believe you. Doesn't change the fact you strapped an explosive to her. Who knows what kind of therapy she's gonna need when she grows up."

"We all do what we must." Vasquez's words lacked conviction. He sighed, toweled off his hands, and seemed to relinquish himself to having this conversation in the men's restroom. "How did you find me?"

"That wasn't too difficult. Did you know Goddard and his assistant, who we have in custody, kept an extremely detailed dossier on you? Right down to how you take your coffee. You should try to stick to only one sugar in every cup. I know you've been stressed lately. Still, three is a bit much, isn't it? Especially on top of the heavy cream. I mean, I love the stuff, but not in my coffee."

Vasquez's mouth drew tight. Jack had him right where he wanted him. When the other man didn't say anything, Jack went for the kill.

"You have no idea how much I want to kill you right now. Luckily for you, you possess skills I'm in need of employing."

"And what skills would those be?" Vasquez's tone was measured. He narrowed his eyes.

"The digging up dirt, finding an ant on a mole-ridden ass on a nude beach full of people with mole-ridden asses, investigative kind." He stopped to grin at Vasquez, who did not return the gesture. Jack shook his head, sighed, continued. "I need some information on a man named Thorne." Jack pulled a piece of paper out of his pocket. It contained all the information they knew about the guy. It wasn't much, but he figured it'd be all Vasquez would need.

Vasquez took the paper but didn't look at it. "And if I don't help you?"

Jack shrugged. "You'll regret it in one way or another. I'm a good man at heart, but don't test my patience. I'm a cold-blooded killer when I'm paid enough. Or pissed enough. I can make your life a living hell."

Vasquez's shoulders slumped, his chin dropped an inch. His expression was easy to read. Jack could see the way he went through all possible scenarios, all possible escape routes. But the former lieutenant knew what Jack knew. If Noble knew something as inconsequential as his coffee order, imagine what he knew that was being left unsaid.

Vasquez gritted his teeth, nodded, and pocketed the paper. It was all the confirmation Jack needed.

"Perfect." Jack wagged his finger at the guy. "And one more thing."

Jack closed his hand into a fist and pulled his arm back. Vasquez had just enough time to register what was happening right before

Jack's fist connected with his nose. There was a satisfying crack as Vasquez's head hit the sink.

Jack shook out his hand, looked the man up and down, and laughed. "I'm expecting a report from you within a week." When he turned and walked away, Jack felt certain Vasquez would find a way to get his revenge, but Noble couldn't bring himself to care.

CHAPTER THIRTY-FIVE

March 29, 2006

Sadie wiped a trickle of sweat off her cheek with her index finger. She stood under a vent just past the ticketing counter. This was her first flight back to the States in three years. She thought she'd be clamoring to get past security and to her boarding gate, all but guaranteeing she'd make her flight home. But there was something left to do.

She saw Bear first. He stood almost a head above the average person. Even those close to his height rarely had his kind of heft. His wide muscular frame helped him carry his weight well. He pulled off his cap and shook his hair free, then patted his beard down. Must've been a windy ride over.

Jack appeared a few seconds later. He stared down at his boarding pass, then looked up at the various counters, finally pointing at their carrier. As she watched him, Sadie wondered what could have been between the two of them if life had led them on different paths. Always practical, she filed the thoughts away in the cabinet marked death bed. And that was a place she hoped she never lingered.

The men greeted her and they made their way through security and into a lounge. They ate and drank and talked and even laughed a couple of times. She wished the moment could be extended on a shared flight, but that was too risky. Vasquez or Thorne could be monitoring their movements. Better for two to survive should one go down. Sadie had a debriefing scheduled in Langley the following morning. The guys would have to meet with Frank soon, too.

After that? Home. Though she wasn't quite sure where that was anymore. Most people didn't understand that sentiment. She was grateful that Jack and Bear weren't most people.

Their conversation died down. Bear stood, pulled out a wad of cash and threw it down. "It's about that time. Better get to my gate." His beard tickled her face as he kissed her on the cheek. "It was real, Sadie. Let's not do it again." He saluted Jack. "We'll get up later."

They watched him exit the lounge and disappear down the corridor. Would she ever see him again? She lifted her beer to her lips and took a pull. Her gaze drifted to the center of the table, then to Jack's hand, and finally to his eyes. They stared at each other for a minute. Neither spoke. She was the first to break it off as she reached into her pocket and added some cash to the pile.

Jack rose with her. He finished off his beer and set it on the table along with his cut of the bill. He jutted his chin toward the exit and they walked out together. They found the middle of the aisle, that place where no one knows quite what to do. Who was meant to walk there? Their pace was slowed. Others stepped aside for them. Sadie wanted to say something, but she wasn't sure what. She stole a glance at Jack and thought she read the same feelings on his face.

He opened his mouth as though to speak.

She cut him off. "It's been interesting."

He nodded. "It has, hasn't it."

"I'm sorry we got off on the wrong foot." She bit her bottom lip.

"Yeah, I'm beginning to think that's the only foot I have anymore."

She glanced over and smiled at him, then went back to staring at the floor in front of them. "I just want to say, thank you."

"For what?"

"When you're under so long, the world around you warps to fit your new perspective. They talk about how character actors get so involved in their projects that they take on the persona in real life. If their character is depressed or demented, they become that way as well. It affects them so badly they sometimes need therapy afterward."

"Are you saying you're gonna need a therapist? Or that I acted as one?"

She forced a laugh and smile. "Trust me, Jack. No one is ever going to mistake you for a therapist."

He shrugged, smiled, said nothing.

She took his hand in hers. He didn't pull away. Their fingers interlaced and he squeezed her hand. "You, both you and Bear, you guys pulled me back in."

He led them to a deserted gate where the lights were off and the seats empty. They stopped in front of a large bank of windows. A 747 taxied to the runway. Was it Bear's? Jack let go of her hand and crossed his arms over his chest.

"What is it?" she asked.

"What did they to do you?"

"Who? The Agency?"

"Goddard and Nicolás?"

Sadie blew a wayward strand of hair out of her face and tucked it behind her ear. She faced the window, crossing her arms to mirror Jack's stance. "Goddard was good to me. It was Mateo that I was afraid of. I started off like anyone else, at the bottom. But I was smart about it. I knew what they wanted from me and what it would take. I had to work my way up quickly so I didn't always do that in the most moral of ways."

"You did what you had to do to get the job done."

She stared at her reflection in the glass as she nodded. The dull image of herself couldn't hide the guilt and remorse she felt over her actions. "Somewhere along the way the line between Michelle and

Sadie blurred. I think I'm always going to have to live with what I, what she did." She tucked her chin to her chest and shook her head.

"Maybe you should see a therapist."

She looked up and returned his smile. "That's the best you can do?"

"We're always learning," he said. "In our line of work, we have to do some terrible things to define the line between right and wrong for others."

She leaned back against the glass and watched the steady stream of travelers wandering through the terminal. Much like in life, they were coming or going and had no idea that the covert underworld was only steps away from them.

"You know, when Goddard took me under his wing, he knew what Mateo had requested of me."

"But he didn't stop him?"

She pulled her hair over her shoulder and leaned back into the glass. It felt cool against her neck and upper back. "It was happening to other women, too. Goddard didn't stop it, but he saved me from it. He saw something different in me, I guess."

"And Nicolás?"

She shook her head. "He was an idiot."

"Did you have feelings for him?" Jack turned sideways, crossed one foot over the other, leaned with his shoulder against the glass.

"I don't think I did." She closed her eyes and heaved a sigh. "Definitely not at first. But as Sadie and Michelle melded into one, I think I developed hope for him. Does that make sense?" She paused a beat. "I never forgot what I was doing there, but I saw something in Nicolás that made him different from the others. Did you notice the way he settled down after he realized there was no escape?"

"Different guy there at the end. I mean, he was cracking jokes with us."

She smiled as a dozen memories ran through her mind's eye in the span of a second or two. "He never wanted this life. His dream was to be an artist. A painter, actually. There's a locked room in that house that only he can enter. It's full of his paintings. But his uncle adopted him, toughened him up, turned him into a mad dog killer. Every once in a while I saw the artist inside him, but he pushed it back down so deep that it almost never came out anymore."

"Most people don't change."

"That's the thing," she said. "I believe they can. They just need to want to change for themselves, not for someone else. Nicolás was just trying to survive. Same as me. The only difference was I was able to hold onto myself."

"And here you are." Jack swept his hand in front of them.

"And here I am." Sadie checked her phone and felt her stomach knot and a wave of sadness pass through her. There were only a few minutes left. "Do you think we'll run into each other again?"

Jack didn't hesitate. "Definitely. We're gonna become best friends, you and me. You're gonna get sick of seeing my ugly mug and dealing with the fleas Bear leaves behind at my place."

Sadie laughed. "Doubtful." She looked up at him and bit her lip. She didn't want to say goodbye. "Walk me to my gate?"

Jack took her bag from her. It was probably like carrying a roll of paper towels to him. Very few possessions from her days as one of Goddard's underlings meant anything to her. She hadn't checked any luggage. The items in the small black duffel would help transition her back to her *old* new life.

"So what'll happen after you're debriefed?" Jack said. "After this they probably can't keep you in covert ops, can they?"

"Doubtful," she said. "At least not any time soon, or without some major reconstructive surgery." She looked over and smiled at him. "Wouldn't that be something? I could stalk you and you'd never know it was me."

He leaned over and sniffed her hair. "Got your scent now. You won't be able to fool me."

"Ah, the wolf. I guess we'll see." She slowed to a stop in front of her gate as the woman behind the counter called the final group for boarding. Jack handed over her bag. She leaned in and kissed him on the cheek, deliberately missing her mark by an inch so that the corners of their lips met. They were sweet and salty with a hint of hops. She had more she wanted to say, but the words would be lost here in Costa Rica. The ripple effect wouldn't carry them back to Langley, or D.C., or New York City.

And perhaps that was for the best.

She gave him a smile and a wink and turned away. She passed the counter and entered the jetway where she was met with hot, humid air. She never looked back at the man named Noble.

Not once.

CHAPTER THIRTY-SIX

C alm washed over Jack as he turned away from Sadie. It felt as though this chapter had been closed. He knew it hadn't, though.

He checked his watch, a Rolex Submariner knock off he'd purchased outside the airport entrance. It looked real enough for the time being. Once back in New York he could put on the real thing if he wanted to. He usually didn't.

He had an hour until his flight would start boarding, so he wandered to his terminal and found an empty bank of seats and laid down on them. His thoughts traveled back over what had happened.

The op had been complicated and convoluted. Nothing new there. They had to trust enemies and watch their backs when friends were around. Nothing new there, either. But the consequences of his actions and inactions were far from over. Sure Goddard was dead, and Camila was safe, and he and Bear were alive. In many ways, that was all that mattered.

But there were other factors now. Sadie, for one. She'd only been gone from his life for a few minutes but the effect had already taken hold of him. He wondered if he had missed on something with her. As to what that was, well he wasn't so sure he wanted to explore that yet. His life was complicated and convoluted and he routinely paid for his actions and inactions. He wasn't meant for anything deeper than something superficial. Sadie deserved better than that.

His zen-like state dissipated as his thoughts traveled to the other factor left to deal with.

Thorne.

Jack pulled the wayfarer sunglasses from his pocket and pulled them down over his eyes. He didn't care for being kept in the dark, and Thorne was as mysterious as anyone he'd met in recent years. And that was saying a lot. The thing that bothered him was the fact that neither he or Bear detected anything when they first encountered the guy. He was Frank's new lackey. So what. How had they not picked up on it?

He debated whether he should call Frank now. Instinct told him Frank had nothing to do with the double cross. Could Frank do something like that? Yes. Would he? Not without good reason, and Jack made it a point not to give the SIS chief a reason. The goal of the op had been to terminate Goddard. As far as Frank would be concerned, the quicker the better. It wouldn't make sense for Frank to cause so much trouble for them.

He sat up and watched a young family, clearly from the States. The wife had a distinct mid-western accent. Wisconsin, maybe. The kid was wearing a Vikings t-shirt, so Jack changed his mind and pegged them from Minnesota. They smiled as they read a book together, completely unaware of the political change Jack had caused.

Would it be for the better? They'd just have to wait to find out.

He leaned back and placed his hands behind his head.

The woman at the counter announced they'd start boarding in ten minutes.

He'd allow himself his flight back to D.C. to rest and catch up on some sleep while trying to clear his mind of the events of the past few days.

Once his feet touched American soil, it was game on. He'd gauge what Frank knew and then go after the turncoat.

Thorne had no idea what the hell he had unleashed upon himself when he'd decided to play puppet master with Jack and Bear.

CHAPTER THIRTY-SEVEN

April 1, 2006

I stepped into the dive off Reeves feeling as though I'd walked into a vat of grease. The smell of beer and pizza and smoke mixed to form an odd aroma that left me starving and gagging at the same time.

Jack sat in a corner booth with a half-full beer and an empty plate stained red in front of him. A mug was perched next to a plate across from him on the table. I passed the row of barstools, all of which were occupied by the kind of people who enjoyed a beer and a slice at ten in the morning.

Jack nodded at me and gestured for me to sit.

"How was your flight?" I slid into the booth.

"Long."

"I hear you, partner." I tried to rub the crick out of my neck. "Turbulence damn near brought my stone shack down around me."

"Any trouble when you got in? Anyone at the airport?"

"Nah. You?"

Jack shook his head. His gaze slid toward the entrance. His face tightened. I didn't have to look back to know that Frank had arrived.

I downed half my beer in a couple gulps and grabbed a slice of pizza off the plate. It was still hot. I breathed in the steam and then took a large bite.

"Now that's good pizza," Jack said. "Thick, cheesy, and greasy. All you need, man."

"You can't make bad pizza." I turned to Frank as he dragged a chair from a nearby table and parked it between us. "Tell him, Frank. You can't make bad pizza."

"There's good pizza and then there's better pizza." Frank shrugged as he looked around the room. "What's a guy gotta do to get a beer around here?"

"Order it yourself." Jack took a long swig of his drink, wiped the head off his upper lip.

Frank stared over at the bar. "Any chance the waitress will actually make it over here any time soon?"

Jack said, "I wouldn't hold your breath."

Frank resigned himself to going up to the crowded bar to order his drink. I leaned forward over the table and kept my voice as low as I could. "What's the plan here? We gonna tell him?"

Jack kept his gaze on the man. "Depends on him. If he acts shady, I ain't sharing shit. Follow my lead, OK?"

I nodded and grabbed the last slice off my plate. Jack knew Frank better than I did. He'd know if Skinner was keeping something from us, even if we weren't sure what that was.

Frank returned and eyed our empty plates and patted his stomach, then stretched one leg over his seat and plopped down. "So what's this about? We could've met in my office. The booze is better there."

"No pizza, though," I said.

"No pizza here either," he said.

"Speak for yourself." I shoved the remainder of the crust in my mouth.

Jack leaned forward over his arms and spoke softly. "Why did you want the senator taken out?"

Frank stiffened, paused, glanced around the room. The bar

wasn't crowded, but it wasn't empty either. We had some distance from the others in our little corner. Springsteen belted out from the jukebox, probably providing enough cover for us to speak openly. It was the kind of place people didn't give a care about others in, and a place that wouldn't be bugged. It's why Jack picked it. Frank should've known that. He just had to be dramatic about his paranoia.

"You don't need me to answer that." Frank smiled, shaking his head. "You telling me you didn't see the evidence plain as day? Come on. Is that even a question?"

Jack glanced at me, back at Frank, nodded. "There were complications."

"What kind of complications?" Frank drew nearer.

"Unaccounted for players," Jack said.

Frank set his glass down with a loud *clunk*. "I don't like unaccounted for players."

"Neither do we," I said. "And yet here we are."

"Who?" Frank glanced between the two of us.

Jack clenched his jaw. The muscles at the corner of his mouth worked in and out. "I don't feel comfortable telling you that just yet."

"You don't trust me?" Frank leaned back, pointed at himself.

"Never have."

"After all this time, Jack?"

"Do you trust me, Frank?"

Frank deadpanned. "Fair point."

We fell silent for a moment. I spoke up. "Have you heard anything?"

"About what?" Frank crossed his arms and expelled a heavy breath. "You haven't told me anything."

"We will, in time," Jack said. "For now, let us know if you've had any suspicions."

"Suspicions?" Frank leaned back and looked up at the ceiling. "You think it's one of my men, don't you?"

"Never said that."

"You're not denying it."

"We're keeping all options on the table."

Frank drained the rest of his drink. "You know my vetting process. You know how hard it is to get something past me. It's damn near impossible."

"Near is not absolute," Jack said. "We need to know if it's a possibility."

Frank crumpled up one of the napkins in his fist and threw it down on the table. "It's always a possibility. But if that's the case, someone else is in on this."

"What do you mean?"

"I mean, you'd have to have pretty strong resources to throw me off your path."

"What kind of resources?"

Frank rubbed his chin. "NSA? CIA? Maybe one of five people in the Pentagon. Someone way up there. And I mean way, way up there."

Jack straightened. "We were working with the CIA down there."

Frank waved his hand. "The girl is a nobody." Frank missed the way Jack's gaze sharpened on him. "Her boss is pretty low level, considering what you're alleging. It'd be way above their pay grade."

I looked over at Jack and said, "Makes sense if it was the CIA, though. They were already entrenched with Goddard way before we got there. Sadie recognized you the day before the hit was supposed to go down. If she reported back to her handler and word got around, there'd be enough time to set up the kidnapping."

"Still trying to figure that one out," Frank said. "No one should've known Javier was involved."

"Well someone did." Jack finished off his drink and caught the eye of a waitress swinging by with an armful of nachos and wings.

"One minute, hon." We all waited until she stopped and grabbed our refill orders before resuming the conversation.

I kept one eye out for her return as I spoke. "If it was the CIA, they'd know, wouldn't they? Sadie and Javier appeared to have formed some kind of working relationship over the years."

"He's assisted her once or twice. It's possible. More than possible. But if that's the case—"

"Then we've got a bigger problem on our hands than we originally thought," Jack said.

The waitress returned with three beers and a complimentary slice of pizza for Frank. He took a bite and downed half of his drink. "Look, you need to tell me what's going on. I can't help you unless you tell me."

Jack looked at me and raised an eyebrow as if to say it was my call.

I shrugged and said, "We need the info."

Frank looked to Jack and waited a beat.

"Camila's kidnapping wasn't Nicolás Garcia's idea. By the time we caught up with him, he pretty much admitted she was dropped in his lap."

"By who?"

Jack ignored the question. "When Vasquez got involved, things got a bit more complicated. But as far as I could tell, he wasn't in on the rest of the plan. He wanted the senator dead from the get-go, and when things started to go sideways, he turned the tables in his favor."

"You know you're gonna have to tell me who was the ones pulling the strings here."

"Where did the op come from?" Jack asked.

Frank licked the grease off his fingertips. "Where they all come from. A source within the Pentagon suggested something be done about someone who was making too many waves. I looked at the situation and made a call. Whoever offered the op in the first place hadn't necessarily wanted him dead, but it was an option. Sometimes blackmail is enough to get the job done. In this case, not so much."

"You didn't think that would be enough this time?"

"No. His empire was too big. He had his hands in too many pots. It would've been impossible to take all of that away from him with a couple of threatening messages."

"Is there a chance that whoever sent you the op didn't actually want you to take him out?"

"It's possible, but again, the discretion was mine. If they didn't want that option on the table, they would've said so."

I took a drink before I spoke. My mouth was still dry from the flight over. "So we're looking at an outside source who had access to this information. Someone who saw the op greenlighted and decided to take matters into their own hands."

"Sounds like it." Frank swirled his glass around. "So tell me who you think it is. That's the only way I'm gonna be able to help."

Jack chewed at the inside of his lip before turning to Frank. "What can you tell us about Daniel Thorne?"

CHAPTER THIRTY-EIGHT

The front door opened and six people walked through. They called out to a few of the patrons at the bar. The bartender smiled and waved them over. Wind blew through the room and sent napkins flying. The whole place seemed to erupt in action.

Except at our table.

Frank was still. So much so I thought he might've died on the spot if it weren't for his eyes blinking. I glanced over at Jack, but he was focused on Frank's face, trying to read the man.

Jack said, "Frank, what is it?"

Frank ignored him. He rocked back in his chair, rose, and turned to the door. "I need to go."

Jack grabbed Frank's arm, stopped him in his tracks. Frank looked back and down at Jack, his eyes narrowed, eyebrows tight together. He wasn't used to people talking back to him, much less *assaulting* him in such a way. Not many people could get away with a reaction like that and live to tell about it. It was different with Jack. Maybe because Noble was one of the few people not afraid of Skinner and the SIS.

"We're the ones who were thrown into the middle of this." He kept his grip tight on Frank's arm. "You owe us an explanation."

Frank ground his teeth but didn't say anything. He sat back down, only resting on the edge of his seat. Jack let go of his arm and eased forward.

"Daniel Thorne was recommended to me by an associate. Someone I actually considered a friend."

Jack said, "Which friend?

Frank said, "That's unimportant."

I stifled a laugh. "The hell it is. That could be the key to all of this."

Frank wagged a finger in my face. "I trust my source."

I smacked it away. "Doesn't mean we do."

Frank clasped his hands together. "But you trust me."

Jack said, "Barely."

"Look, the source is clean. I'd trust him with my life, no questions asked. It's an old friend, from way back."

"Whoever it is, they sent you a double-agent."

Frank shook his head. "Not intentionally." Jack made to say something else, but Frank put up a hand. "We can get into it more later, but just trust me on this for right now. The source is clean, even if Thorne isn't."

I glanced at Jack and he nodded. We'd let it go, for the moment. But Frank was kidding himself if he thought we weren't going to have a long discussion about this so-called source at some point soon.

"All right," Jack said. "Tell us everything you know about Thorne?"

Frank glanced around the room, perhaps to reassess the current clientele. They must've passed his eyeball test. "Military brat. Enlisted when he was eighteen. Marines. Reminds me a bit of you, Jack. Hard-headed, stubborn, a pain in the ass. Smart, though. Tactical, cunning, resourceful. Has the ability to spin a story like you wouldn't believe. Not as good of a fighter or a shot as the two of you, but you could send him into any situation and he'd talk his way out of it without throwing a single punch and then whoever pissed him off, he'd shoot them in the back."

I figured there was a warning there. "He didn't seem all too charismatic when we met him."

"That's part of his act, trust me. He knew who you were, Jack. Knew both of you. He volunteered to bring you the dossier on the senator."

Jack leaned back to take it in. "And that didn't seem strange to you?"

"He'd been restless for a while now. You know what that building is like when you're stuck in it for a few weeks straight. He'd taken a couple odd jobs here and there, but there was a lot of downtime. Happens sometimes, right? Anyway, he'd done drop-offs like that for me before. I didn't think anything of it."

"You underestimated him."

"I'm fully aware."

The waitress swung by our table, this time carrying a pint of beer and burger with fries meant for someone else. Frank requested the check. She gave him a quick nod and sped on past.

Jack waited until she was gone before he spoke again. "What would he want with the senator? Goddard mentioned a pipeline?"

Frank's eyes narrowed. "It was one of his biggest projects. One of the reasons why someone wanted him taken out was because he was getting too greedy. He had half the senate in his pocket. The other half wasn't too happy about it."

"So someone in the Senate set up the job?"

Frank wagged his finger. "Don't play guessing games. You'll be wrong every time."

"No, you just won't tell me when I'm right."

"Still. There's no point in trying to figure out who set it up. The fact is we know why." Frank snapped his mouth shut as the waitress arrived with the check. He waited until she walked away then continued. "Now we just have to figure out the why for Thorne." He paused a beat. "There could be a million reasons Thorne wanted that pipeline to go through. Maybe he has a stake in it. Maybe he was hired." Franked tilted his head in Jack's direction. "That last one is very likely. Like I said, he's been getting antsy lately."

I rose and stepped out from the booth. "So where do we find him?"

Frank crossed his arms. "The chances of him coming into the office tomorrow are slim, I'm sure. In fact I'm thinking he might not ever return."

Jack joined me behind Frank. Skinner didn't look back at us. Jack said, "Anytime you want to be helpful, Frank, let us know."

He lowered his head and shook it. "Look, you don't know this guy's background. Thorne is good."

Jack placed one hand on the corner of the table and leaned forward to speak right in Frank's ear. "We're better."

"I'm not gonna argue that, but it doesn't negate the fact that he's still good. If he doesn't want to be found, he's going to make it pretty damn hard on us. I'll devote some resources to it, but you may have to reach out to other contacts."

Jack waved a hand. "We're already on it."

Frank raised an eyebrow. "Who?"

"Someone who dealt with this firsthand."

"Don't tell me you're leaning on Vasquez. I know he's good, but you think that's the smart move?"

"Absolutely," Jack said. "Vasquez is an untapped resource. He's also expendable."

"Thorne also knows you've been in contact with him."

"He doesn't know we've become friendly, though."

Frank pushed his drink away, the anger on his face palpable. "I keep telling you not to underestimate him, Jack. When are you going to listen?"

"Probably never."

"It's your funeral."

"It'll be yours, too," I said. "You started this mess, Frank. You're gonna help us figure out how to clean it up."

Frank made to say something else, but Jack didn't let him. "You're gonna get the check right? You can probably deduct it as a work meeting. I'd say that's fair."

We left Frank sitting there, seething on our crumbs. Somehow it'd come back on us. Until then, I enjoyed it.

CHAPTER THIRTY-NINE

June 14th, 2006

I stood inside a used bookstore on an aisle that contained four rows of nudie magazines and eight dedicated to gardening. Guess it was all relative. It smelled like mildew and corn chips. Oddly enough, that turned my stomach a little. Across the street Jack occupied a bistro table under a cherry tree. He held a mug of coffee in one hand, a newspaper in the other. Thorne's wayfarers were perched on his nose. Anyone passing by might guess Noble hadn't a care in the world. They were only partially right. It was just that his cares were more complex than the average person.

I heard everything going on around him through my earpiece.

It was a perfect New York City day. One better spent in a park, watching the college girls jog by in their short shorts. Instead we were waiting on Thorne.

We'd dedicated the past two months to tracking him at the cost of everything else. Jack had turned down seven figures in contracts. The process hadn't been an easy one. We had to keep our distance throughout most of it.

Until now.

The chase went from hot to stale frequently. The closer we got, the further Thorne slipped away. The periods of inactivity grew longer. Nothing about his actions indicated he was on to us, rather this was how he lived now. Maybe because he'd spurred Frank, though Skinner felt that Thorne had ample protection and had no need to fear the reach of the SIS.

Frank was right about many things. Thorne was extremely careful, dropping off the face of the earth it seemed.

If it hadn't been for Vasquez, we might never have made it this far. He'd first spotted him in Spain. Then in Moscow. We'd followed the trail to both places, but by the time we landed, Thorne had vanished. Week after week the process repeated itself. Frankfurt. Delhi. Tokyo. Melbourne. Copenhagen. Thorne remained a step or two ahead.

Until he decided to return to our home turf. Vasquez pinned him in New York and this time it appeared Thorne had extended business here. With who and for what, we had no idea. And we didn't care.

I felt we were jumping the gun by moving so fast. All intelligence we had gathered said we had more time. Jack wanted to make an impression. He wanted Thorne to know we were close. Not the smartest move, but restless minds prevailed over patience.

Through a well-placed network of homeless people a la *Sherlock Holmes*, Jack learned that Thorne had a meeting with an unknown contact at this restaurant. Jack sat in plain sight, not bothering to disguise himself. He was positive Thorne wouldn't run. Why should he? We were in Manhattan. There were people and cameras everywhere. Nothing would happen. And Thorne could take the opportunity to rub it in Jack's face that he had eluded them for so long.

Thorne strolled out onto the patio, a smile on his face. He nodded at Jack and then reached out and caught the waitress. He leaned in and spoke to her. She smiled at him, and walked off with her pen to her pad. Thorne watched her walk away, then headed straight for Jack. He pulled out the chair and sat down. The guy was at ease.

The hair on the back on my neck stood on end.

Jack's breathing quickened.

"Hello, Jack."

"Thorne."

"I believe those are my sunglasses."

Jack adjusted them on his face. "Yeah, but they look so much better on me."

Thorne pulled a new pair from his breast pocket. "You know what, they do. Why don't you keep them."

The waitress brought Thorne his drink. She hovered there for a minute before he finally dismissed her with a gesture of his hand. The man took a languid sip before crossing his legs and hooking an arm over the back of his chair. Mr. Casual just enjoying a morning drink with a friend.

"Why don't you tell Riley to come on out, Jack?"

"I'm alone. There's no need to be paranoid."

"Paranoid keeps me alive. I'm sure you can relate." Thorne pointed out toward the bookstore. "He's in there. I saw him go in an hour ago."

Jack glanced up at the high-rises then looked in my direction. He hesitated a beat, then nodded. I left the lookout, crossed the street, and joined them at the table.

"You want a drink, Riley?" Thorne held his glass up to me.

"I'm good."

Thorne took another sip. "Suit yourself."

"You knew we were here." Jack didn't ask it as a question.

"Of course I did. You've been following me for months. You think this was a lucky break?" He air-quoted the last two words.

Jack and I exchanged a look. Both of us hated when people used air quotes.

Thorne smiled, lifting his index finger off his glass and pointing at us. "You did, didn't you. Look, boys, no offense, but you're not as good as you think you are. Better than most?" He held up his other hand and teetered it side to side. "Maybe. You shouldn't have been able to find me at all, so kudos to you. I gotta tell you, I was getting sick of bouncing around every few days. That's why I came back here. I can handle the fallout here so much better than in another country."

"We know what you're up to, Thorne," Jack said. "It's time to come in."

Thorne's smile lingered. "You two have no idea what I'm up to. You know I wanted Goddard dead, but you still have no idea why. And you won't ever know. I recommend you give up trying to figure it out."

"If you knew us as well as you thought you did, you'd realize we're too stupid to give up even when all the evidence points to it being the right thing to do."

"You did your job," Thorne said. "You got paid. Why do you even care? Do you need a gold sticker on your chart, too? Well, gosh, I'll make sure to put one on there next time I'm visiting the Pentagon."

"I don't like being played."

"Get used to it, Jack. You're not going to win this one. And if you keep trying, I'm going to be compelled to start interfering in your business. Would you like that? Do you want me snooping around, getting involved?"

"You don't know me," Jack said. "You only think you do."

"I know you better than you think I do." Thorne drained his glass and rose. He faced the breeze, closed his eyes and breathed deeply as he dropped a couple bills on the table. "Drink's on me, Jack. Enjoy."

I hopped up and blocked Thorne's path. "You're not leaving."

Thorne looked around. "There's literally a hundred ways for me to go here. You can't stop me, Riley."

"Bet on it."

"I would, but you'd lose."

"Bear." Jack's voice told me something was wrong.

I glanced over to see Jack staring at my chest. "Should I have brought you a few of those magazines?"

He said nothing. Shook his head. Kept staring.

I glanced down and saw trio of red dots dancing across my torso. For some reason I stopped breathing.

Thorne patted my chest and lifted an eyebrow. "Like I said, you'd lose."

Jack stood slowly. "We're not going to stop tracking you down, Thorne. You can bet on that."

Thorne shook his head. "Even with your partner moments from death, you still can't stop. My God, I'd marry you if I was into that kind of thing." He turned and took a few steps. "Just remember, Jack, I can't be held responsible for the consequences you'll endure. Have you spoken to Sadie, by the way? How's she doing?"

"You leave her out of this. This is between us."

Thorne held up his hands in surrender and backed away. "Just a friendly question, Jack. But something to keep in mind." Thorne turned and walked toward the small iron gate, tossing one more comment over his shoulder as he stepped over it. "Those glasses really do look better on you. I hope they're not the only thing you take away from this."

THE END

Thorne hasn't seen the last of Bear & Noble! Bear will be back to deal with him in Blowback, now available for preorder here:

https://ltryan.com/bear-logan-blowback-preorder/

Until then, catch up on their adventures in the Jack Noble series - Links for all books below!

Want to be among the first to download the next Jack Noble book? Sign up for L.T. Ryan's newsletter, and you'll be notified the minute new releases are available - and often at a discount for the first 48 hours! As a thank you for signing up, you'll receive a complimentary copy of *The Recruit: A Jack Noble Short Story.*

Join here: http://ltryan.com/newsletter/

I enjoy hearing from readers. Feel free to drop me a line at ltryan70@gmail.com. I read and respond to every message.

If you enjoyed reading *A Deadly Distance*, I would appreciate it if you would help others enjoy these books, too. How?

Lend it. This e-book is lending-enabled, so please, feel free to share it with a friend. All they need is an amazon account and a Kindle, or Kindle reading app on their smart phone or computer.

Recommend it. Please help other readers find this book by recommending it to friends, readers' groups and discussion boards.

Review it. Please tell other readers why you liked this book by reviewing it at Amazon, Barnes & Noble, Apple or Goodreads. Your opinion goes a long way in helping others decide if a book is for them. Also, a review doesn't have to be a big old book report. If you do write a review, please send me an email at ltryan70@gmail.com so I can thank you with a personal email.

Like Jack. Visit the Jack Noble Facebook page and give it a like: https://www.facebook.com/JackNobleBooks.

ALSO BY L.T. RYAN

The Jack Noble Series

The Recruit (free)

The First Deception (Prequel 1)

Noble Beginnings

A Deadly Distance

Ripple Effect (Bear Logan)

Thin Line

Noble Intentions

When Dead in Greece

Noble Retribution

Noble Betrayal

Never Go Home

Beyond Betrayal (Clarissa Abbot)

Noble Judgment

Never Cry Mercy

Deadline

End Game

Mitch Tanner Series

The Depth of Darkness

Into The Darkness

Deliver Us From Darkness - coming soon

Affliction Z Series

ABOUT THE AUTHOR

L.T. Ryan is a *USA Today* and international bestselling author. The new age of publishing offered L.T. the opportunity to blend his passions for creating, marketing, and technology to reach audiences with his popular Jack Noble series.

Living in central Virginia with his wife, the youngest of his three daughters, and their three dogs, L.T. enjoys staring out his window at the trees and mountains while he should be writing, as well as reading, hiking, running, and playing with gadgets. See what he's up to at http://ltryan.com.

Social Medial Links:

- Facebook (L.T. Ryan): https://www.facebook.com/LTRyanAuthor

- Facebook (Jack Noble Page): https://www.facebook.com/JackNobleBooks/

- Twitter: https://twitter.com/LTRyanWrites

- Goodreads: http://www.goodreads.com/author/show/6151659.L_T_Ryan

92698022R00158

Made in the USA
San Bernardino, CA
04 November 2018